A W Faber-Castell

The Magic Pencil 5

The Magic Pencil 5

tellwell

Tellwell Talent
www.tellwell.ca

ISBN
978-0-2288-8089-9 (Hardcover)
978-0-2288-8088-2 (Paperback)
978-0-2288-8090-5 (eBook)

A pencil is a powerful magic weapon for good.

Author: Count Andreas Wilhelm von Faber-Castell

For author A.W. Faber-Castell (Count Andreas von Faber-Castell), every pencil holds the promise of magic. From the time he was a young boy he has always regarded pencils as small magic wands that inspire creativity and make the imagination visible.

Known as Count Andy to his colleagues, he is the last surviving member of the 8th generation pencil dynasty to have been actively involved in the running of the famous company, which began in Germany in 1761.

Andy was the company's undisputed champion for developing children's products – the main contributor to Faber-Castell's success over recent decades. One of his claims to fame was the launch of his beloved Connector Pen. He was its sole champion initially, but with passion and persistence he ultimately brought the disbelievers in the company on board. The pen became famous worldwide, and it has been the number one colouring product in Australia for the past twenty-five years.

Captain Klump

Hermann and Fritz

Roger Less

Michaela

Andy

Sally and Sassy

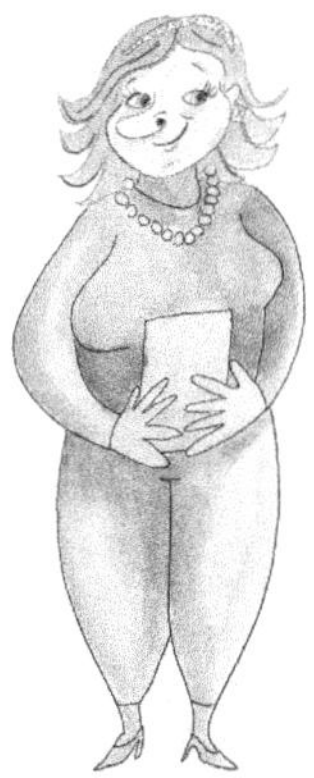

Lady Heger-Steel

Commander and Mrs Wurstling

Anna

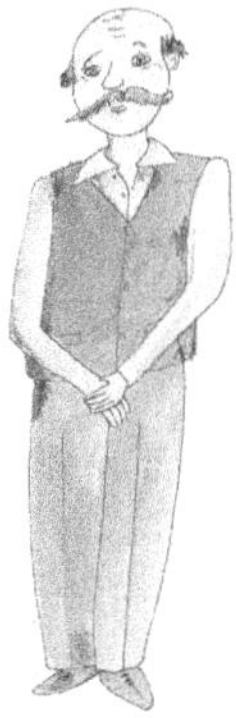

Johann

Kunnikunde

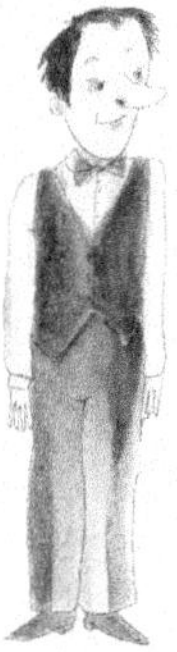

Rollover von Cracklingen

Mr Broombridge

Lucifer

Dr. Ulrich Folterknecht

Ido Farkheem

General Mambo

Idi Amonia

Table of Contents

Chapter One 1
Chapter Two 5
Chapter Three 8
Chapter Four 13
Chapter Five 17
Chapter Six 21
Chapter Seven 24
Chapter Eight 27
Chapter Nine 31
Chapter Ten 35
Chapter Eleven 39
Chapter Twelve 44
Chapter Thirteen 49
Chapter Fourteen 54
Chapter Fifteen 57
Chapter Sixteen 63
Chapter Seventeen 67
Chapter Eighteen 72
Chapter Nineteen 76
Chapter Twenty 80

Chapter Twenty-One 84
Chapter Twenty-Two 87
Chapter Twenty-Three 91
Chapter Twenty-Four 93
Chapter Twenty-Five 98
Chapter Twenty-Six 103
Chapter Twenty-Seven 108
Chapter Twenty-Eight 113

1

'I am broke!' Countess Kunnikunde Ritter von Krumm screeched at her three advisory board members from the big video conferencing screen mounted on the boardroom wall. 'This company—my company—is bankrupt! I'm ruined . . . all because of you! Your incompetence is second to none! You are complete morons!'

Kunnikunde's ear-splitting rant reverberated through the old Ritter von Krumm pencil company, making it clear to everyone in the building what she thought of her senior executives.

With morale at the failing pencil company already at an all-time low, shouting abuse at her management team was a questionable leadership tactic.

'But Aunt Kunnikunde,' Rollover von Cracklingen bravely said, 'We are trying our best! Right at this moment, Mr Broombridge is finalising the sale of substantial properties in order to prop up our profit. We also have two parties keen to buy your company! We should finalise a deal within the next nine months. Please trust us!' He reached out to turn down the volume before she could reply but lost his nerve.

'Trust? Ha!' Kunnikunde hissed into the microphone at her home in Snobtown. 'I don't trust anyone—least of all you useless idiots!' She then switched from hissing back to screeching, this time in a crude Teutonian dialect: '*Iik muss dass makken!*' Her board members had heard it countless times and knew it to mean 'I have to do everything myself!' They watched her larger-than-life face on the big screen twist into a contorted expression of such savage fury that her eyes rolled back in her head.

'We have all made our mistakes, Aunty,' he courageously stated. He then took a very deep breath. 'But you made the biggest one yourself by firing your brother-in-law, Johann. He was a true leader and a great motivator for everyone. And as we now know, in his own new pencil company he is a brilliant creative director and a genius in product development. If you hadn't sacked him, our company would be more successful than ever.'

'Shunned! He is shunned!' Kunnikunde snarled. 'Do not ever mention his name again! Never ever! I will deal with that part of the family, and I have powerful friends who will help me do it! No mistakes this time!'

Cracklingen had heard enough. He pulled the power plug from the wall. The big screen went black as the video conferencing system shut down.

'Rollover!' Farty Ritter von Krumm cried out. 'What are you doing?'

'You shouldn't have done that!' Mr Broombridge yelped.

'That's right!' Kunnikunde's voice rang out from behind Rollover, Farty and Mr Broombridge, who were still facing the blank screen. They almost fell off their chairs when they turned to see their boss standing there.

'It's just a hologram!' declared Cracklingen, putting on a brave face. A second later, that face took the full force of an almighty slap from an angry Kunnikunde, painfully letting Rollover know she was no hologram.

'Rollover!' Kunnikunde shouted into her nephew's now red, stinging face. 'You have turned into a monster! We need to talk soon! I have acquired new powers beyond your imaginings! This time I have convinced my master Lucifer to leave everything to me and for him to stay out of it. And there will be no interference or interruptions by bungling idiots such as Werner Little Werner and you three stooges! Soon you will read in the papers of a tragic, fatal accident that befell three of my family members with me subsequently inheriting their wealth and pencil company.' Kunnikunde then plugged the power cable back into the wall socket and vanished back to her home in Snobtown. An instant later, she was back up on the big screen, this time wearing a cheery and charming smile. The boardroom fell silent. Her three board directors were too stunned to speak. Kunnikunde thanked them all and closed the meeting. This time the screen faded to black without any intervention from Rollover, who was still rubbing his face.

'Oh my God!' he gasped, breaking the silence. 'She's turned into a witch! This is insane!'

'Hah!' Farty retorted. 'My cousin was born a witch—no surprise there for me! She was probably born insane as well!'

'Stop!' shouted Mr Broombridge, the only one of the three not related to Kunnikunde. He was probably hoping his beloved countess was still listening in. 'Do not bad-mouth our great leader!'

Unfortunately for Mr Broombridge, Kunnikunde had lost interest in her board directors' opinion of her. At that very moment, she was walking from the study into the lounge room at her home in Snobtown, visibly satisfied with her show-off performance during the video conference. Waiting for her in the lounge was a young man dressed in a black jacket, white shirt, red trousers, white socks and shiny black shoes. His pale face contrasted starkly with his pitch-black hair. There was no question as to who this striking, confident young man was; he was none other than Lucifer, the devil himself.

'Do you think it was wise to show off your new powers so soon?' the devil asked Kunnikunde.

'You see!' Kunnikunde erupted. 'This is your problem, Lucifer! You over-analyze and complicate everything rather than just getting on and doing the job! When you have powers, use them! Show them off! Intimidate! My approach is simple . . . uncomplicated! I will go over to my brother-in-law's place and wait until the three of them are together—which they frequently are—and I will shake Johann and Anna's hand so I can copy their signatures. Then I will kill them and their rat of a son. After that, I will write their last will and testament for them, sign it with their signatures and bingo! . . . I will inherit it all!'

'I must admit that does sound simple,' Lucifer remarked. 'Maybe too simple.'

Kunnikunde rolled her eyes, shook her head and sighed with exasperation. 'I have so many incredible powers to call on . . . lightning cloud, super speed, laser bombing capacity and teleportation skills! No one could compete with me!'

'Your nephew, Andy,' the devil pointed out. 'He is somehow powerful. Not like a real warrior spirit, but he definitely needs to be trapped. I will provide you with my latest trap . . . just to make sure you're successful in capturing him.'

2

Lucifer and Kunnikunde spent some time discussing the trap for Andy and studying the layout of her brother-in-law Johann's residence in the village of Stone, the chosen location for her planned killing spree.

As it happened, at that precise moment Count Johann's house in Stone was all hustle and bustle. Suitcases were piled up at the front of the house and Johann's son, Andy, was busily loading them into a hired limousine. His mother, Countess Anna, was issuing final house-sitting and pet-minding instructions to their friends Hermann the plumber and Fritz the painter.

'I know I can rely on you both to look after our home while we are away,' Anna said.

'You just enjoy your visit to your sister's, Countess Anna; don't worry about a thing,' Hermann assured her. 'Fritz and I will take care of everything.'

'Oh yes, indeed, Countess!' Fritz said. 'We will treat it as if it were our own place.'

Having seen both their homes Anna wasn't sure that was such a reassuring commitment, but she knew what Fritz meant.

'I have total confidence in you both,' Anna declared with a brave smile.

Andy couldn't wait to hand the house over to Hermann and Fritz and get under way. He and his father were participating in an overseas expedition, organised by the university, to a world-famous national nature park. Andy could barely contain his excitement. His prime objective was to observe wild animals in their natural habitat, while Johann wanted to study trees to find those most suitable for planting as future pencil wood. Adding to Andy's excitement was the fact that it would be his first trip overseas. The only dampener on his enthusiasm was that his girlfriend, Sophia, couldn't join him. Her parents considered it would be too dangerous and refused her permission to go. If Andy could have seen the future, he would have been impressed with the wisdom of their decision.

When Andy and his parents finally drove off, Hermann and Fritz were waving goodbye, but all Andy could see were the sad looks on the faces of his two dogs, Sassy and Sally. For a moment, the thought of leaving them behind made him sad too, but he knew they would be well cared for by Hermann and Fritz.

Once he and his father had dropped Anna off at the train station and she was on her way north to the big city of Burg, Andy was as happy as could be thinking about the adventure ahead. But he had to be patient because it would take them nearly seven hours of driving to reach the harbour where the *MS Teutonia,* a mid-size luxury cruise ship, was docked and ready to take them overseas. During the drive, Andy contacted the spirit of his magic pencil hoping to have a chat, but all he got was the terse response 'I'm busy! Will catch up with you soon' followed by silence. This made Andy nervous. It had now been well over a year since the devil and his lizard-man assassin had tried to murder him, and Andy could feel in his bones that Lucifer was going to try again very soon.

Since that failed attempt, Andy hadn't needed to use his superpowers and worried that he was so out of practice that he wouldn't be able to properly defend himself if he were attacked again. The only special gift he had used in the past year was the animal love gene, which came in handy when he was diagnosing sick residents of the zoo. As a matter of fact, the zookeepers no longer bothered to call on the head veterinarian Professor Katz-Kopf to deal with ill or injured animals and instead went directly to Andy. Out of respect for the professor, Andy always kept him informed and the two developed a close friendship. Of course, Professor Katz-Kopf still called Andy 'Dolittle' after Dr Dolittle, the famous book and movie character who could talk to animals. As it happened, the nickname stuck and most of Andy's fellow veterinary students and all of the zookeepers now also referred to him as Dolittle. Andy was relieved and thankful that his magic pencil didn't call him that as well.

Right now, though, Andy wasn't thinking about his nickname. Despite his disappointment at not being able to talk to the pencil, he realised there was no need to be nervous or worried. In the year since he had avoided being assassinated, his magic pencil hadn't materialised as Michaela. It only seemed to do so when there was a crisis looming. So, everything must be in order, Andy reassured himself. The pencil will warn me if Lucifer is on the warpath again.

All thoughts of future assassination attempts dissipated when he and his father, Johann, arrived at the dock. Andy gazed up at the *MS Teutonia* in awe. Never in his wildest imaginings had he ever expected to sail on a vessel so large and beautiful as the magnificent cruise ship that now towered above him. Once on board, Andy felt he had entered the most luxurious hotel in the world. Standing on the highly polished marble floor of the palatial lobby, he marvelled at the beautiful furniture and magnificent pictures on the walls. He could see stairs going in every direction and an array of elevators serving the many floors. Andy's astonishment grew even more when he took one of those elevators up to his cabin. The cabin was light and bright with a massive bed and en-suite. It even had its own balcony. Andy threw himself onto the bed with sheer delight and lay back thinking how lucky he was. His only regret was that his two dogs weren't there to share this experience with him; he knew Sassy and Sally would have loved nestling up to him on such a huge bed.

3

Andy was jolted out of his thoughts of Sassy and Sally by the sound of loud sirens announcing a safety drill. Once the drill was finished Andy took himself on a discovery tour, inspecting the pool, various decks and many shops surrounding the lobby. He counted three restaurants and two bars offering a great variety of food and drinks.

As Andy walked through the buffet restaurant, he heard a familiar voice shout out, 'Andy! What are you doing here?' Andy turned to see his hometown of Stone's police chief, Commander Wurstling, and his wife seated at a table close by.

'Hello, Commander . . . Mrs Wurstling,' Andy said, approaching their table. He was surprised to see no sausage rolls on the commander's plate. When he explained his presence on the ship, the commander returned the favour.

'I'm taking sugar blossom here on her first ocean cruise,' he said, putting his arm affectionately around Mrs Wurstling.

It was the first time Andy had seen the Stone police chief resplendent in lederhosen and a garish Hawaiian shirt. But what really intrigued him was the fact that Mrs Wurstling was wearing a bulky, bright-red life jacket. He couldn't help staring at it.

'Just in case the ship starts sinking,' Mrs Wurstling explained, answering the question in Andy's wide eyes.

Right at that moment, the ship's engines started, and the ship moved slightly. With a piercing scream, the police commander's sugar blossom almost jumped out of her skin. She ended up in her husband's lederhosen-clad lap, shivering with fright.

Excusing himself, Andy rushed to the top deck to watch the huge vessel slowly leave the busy harbour and head out towards the open sea. He was pumped with excitement and happiness now that he was really off on the sixteen-day cruise to Kinkanza, home of the nation's world-famous Kinkanza Nature Park. Professor Katz-Kopf and Andy's fellow students, arriving by plane, would reach Kinkanza a day earlier than the *MS Teutonia*. Once Andy joined them, they would all spend nine days at a campsite in the park as guests of the local rangers and the University of Kinkanza.

As Andy returned to the lower decks, he bumped into his father who suggested he join him at the Forward Bar behind the pool. The moment they walked into the large bar, Johann was greeted by a familiar voice. 'Hello, old chap. Can I buy you a drink?'

'Roger!' Johann gasped with surprise and delight. 'What are you doing here?'

'Partly holiday, partly a little job I have to do in Kinkanza,' replied Roger Less, the famous agent of Britonnia's Secret Service. He smiled broadly. 'You told me you would be on this ship, so I decided to join you rather than fly direct to Kinkanza. Come, we'll go and sit on the lounge chairs by that large window facing the sea.'

Andy could see that his father was over the moon to have one of his best friends keep him company on the cruise. Andy was also happy to see Roger; the secret agent was like family. And Andy loved hearing about his thrilling adventures—especially when they were about the good guy Roger winning the fight against the forces of evil. Andy had experienced plenty of his own fights against the ultimate forces of evil—otherwise known as his horrible, horrendous Aunt Kunnikunde and the prince of darkness, Lucifer himself.

As Andy started to recall some of his epic battles and narrow escapes, he was distracted by the extraordinary sight of Mrs Wurstling entering the bar with her husband, the commander. His 'sugar blossom' had caught the attention of everyone else as well. To her big bright-red life vest, Mrs Wurstling had added an even larger life-saver ring that she had wedged down firmly on her big stomach and over-sized hips. To Andy, she looked more like a walking anchor buoy than a human being. It was clear the poor lady was still panicked by the thought that the ship would sink at any moment.

'Sugar Blossom!' Commander Wurstling declared. 'I shall order you a triple portion of chocolate mud cake with your tea! You know how rich food always calms you down. And don't forget to keep taking those anti-anxiety pills the doctor prescribed for you.'

After the Wurstlings had greeted Andy, Johann and Roger, they sat down on two lounge chairs right next to them, which creaked alarmingly but held fast. The creaking was instantly replaced by a crackling from the loudspeakers in the bar. Captain Klump's voice rang loudly welcoming his passengers on board and outlining the trip, explaining that the next stop would be the town of Porto where the last passengers would join the ship on their travels to Kinkanza. He told them how proud he was of his ship, and then invited everyone to the captain's dinner the following evening where he would introduce them all to his crew.

No sooner had the loudspeakers gone silent than Andy was startled by another voice, but one that only he could hear. 'Are we having a good time?' the magic pencil asked inside Andy's head.

Recovering quickly, Andy replied brightly, 'Very much so!'

'Good!' the pencil responded. 'Seeing as I'm responsible for you and Johann being on this cruise, I'm glad you're enjoying it.'

'What?' Andy exclaimed. 'What do you mean you're responsible?'

'By manipulating his mind, I caused Professor Katz-Kopf to arrange the whole thing,' the magic pencil responded.

'Why?'

'I needed you all out of Stone for a while . . . for your own protection. Lucifer has turned your Aunt Kunnikunde into a powerful demon. She is now a fully-fledged satanic assassin with only one goal: the elimination of your family.'

'Nothing new!' Andy retorted. 'She has always wanted to destroy us—and almost did, several times!'

'Yes,' the pencil agreed, 'but for the first time she has been equipped with all the powers needed to do the job herself, and she is very determined to succeed.'

'So, what do you want me to do?' Andy asked.

'Sit back, relax, and follow my orders. There are other demons after us too, but we should be able to handle them easily enough. And Lucifer is too busy trying to influence President Numbskull of the New Colonies into starting a war, so we should be able to fly under his radar.'

'So, nothing should happen during our cruise,' Andy said.

'Well, not for at least four days,' the pencil responded. 'However, some of the passengers we pick up in Porto are nothing but trouble. I'm informed by the spirits they will try to take over the ship and hand it to a rogue nation.'

Andy actually smiled to himself at the thought of some action. He had begun wondering what he would do on the ship for two weeks. Despite its luxury and comfort, he knew he would soon find the cruise quite boring. 'So, until something starts happening, what are you going to do?' he asked.

'I will join you on your holiday!' the magic pencil said. 'I've always wanted to travel on a ship like this!'

Moments later the pencil materialised into its human guise, entering the bar as the beautiful Michaela. What an appearance she made, dressed futuristically in a black outfit with silver trimmings. She caught the attention of almost everyone in the bar. Andy was delighted to see her.

His father, Johann, was not. Johann had just taken a sip of wine and nearly choked on it when he saw Michaela. 'Oh no! Oh no! Oh no! No! No! No!' he cried. He turned to Mrs Wurstling, the walking anchor buoy. 'You're right! You're right! We will be sinking—possibly the life rafts too!'

Mrs Wurstling was right in the middle of eating her triple helping of chocolate mud cake to relieve her anxiety. Her current mouthful of cake shot out of her mouth and hit her husband, who was sitting opposite her, full in the face. Before he realised what had happened, his wife had fainted where she sat, slumping forward face-first into the rest of the mud cake on her plate.

'Calm down, sir! Calm down!' Michaela told Johann. 'I'm on holiday too. I can assure you we won't be sinking!'

Johann only calmed down very gradually. Roger wasn't particularly happy seeing Michaela again either, remembering that during their last encounter she had turned him into a goat. He firmly demanded that there be no repeat of such a humiliating experience.

'Of course not, Roger,' Michaela replied sweetly. 'There is no need for me to turn you into a goat anymore.'

Roger looked satisfied, but only briefly because he slowly started to understand the insulting double meaning of her remark.

But before Roger had time to rebut, Andy was jumping up and embracing Michaela. For him, it was like a long-lost sister had come home. They spent a short time in the bar and then proceeded to stroll around the decks, with Michaela showing interest in everything. It was late into the evening when Michaela returned to the magic pencil as a spirit and Andy went to bed feeling very happy. He fell asleep immediately.

4

Sirens were blaring in Snobtown in the New Colonies as every available fire truck raced to attend to five mansions engulfed in flames. One burning close to the centre of town belonged to Pipi von Rotzhausen, a distant relative of Countess Kunnikunde's, whom she disliked because he had money. The other four properties on fire were in a different part of town: coincidentally, Kunnikunde's neighbourhood.

An angry devil suddenly appeared in the countess's lounge room. 'Have you gone completely mad?' he shouted. 'Can you, just once, listen to my instructions? You destroyed the houses of three senators and a congressman! All my people! And worse still, even the home of Pipi von Rotzhausen . . . a good man! He is corrupt, greedy and selfish—a true servant of mine!'

Kunnikunde started to act like a five-year-old girl. 'Hi, hi, hi,' she chirped. 'I needed to test my new powers! Now I know that I'm not only capable of eliminating Johann and his appalling family but also of destroying the whole town of Stone! Ha! Ha! Ha!'

'Kunnikunde!' the devil shrieked. 'That was not in our plan! I am entrusting you to do one job and one job only—to get rid of your disgusting brother-in-law Johann and his family. Johann is the worst kind of human! He cares about the environment, pays fair wages and gives a lot of support to those obnoxious Red Cross and Salvation Army organisations. He's a true enemy of mine! He must be eliminated!'

'Consider it done,' Kunnikunde cooed in her most charming voice.

'It's done when it's done, and not before!' the devil yelled. 'Due to your chronic disobedience, Kunnikunde, I have no choice but to limit your powers. You now have only six laser bombs left—just enough to complete your assignment. And I am also cutting your teleportations to a maximum of ten, which will ensure you focus on the job at hand. You will still have the assistance of the lightning cloud, a formidable weapon in itself . . . also an effective information tool for me. I will know every move you make since the cloud is in steady contact with me!'

'What a breach of privacy!' Kunnikunde pouted. 'Not the way to treat a poor, lonely widow.'

'You are not poor!' shouted the devil. 'The only poor thing about you is your character! As a matter of fact, there is only one woman richer than you in the world—the Queen of Britonnia.'

'Ah ha!' screeched Kunnikunde. 'You admit it! You admit it! I am poor! There is someone richer than me! Is that fair? Is that fair?'

The devil was speechless. Shaking his head in exasperation, he disappeared into thin air. Kunnikunde instantly started wailing about the limits he had put on her and called out to her two daughters, Pink and Rose, seeking sympathy.

Back in Stone, Rollover von Cracklingen and Count Farty Ritter von Krumm were wrestling with the dilemma of whether or not they should warn Johann about Kunnikunde's reappearance. After prolonged discussion, they finally agreed to discreetly do the right thing. This was a new experience for them both, and probably explained why it took them so long to reach that decision.

Fronting up at Johann's house they were very surprised to learn their uncle was on a cruise holiday and that neither of the house sitters, Fritz nor Hermann, could give them the date of his return.

'In about six weeks,' Hermann said. 'But we're not sure.'

Quite unreasonably, the fact that his uncle would go on an extended holiday upset Farty a great deal. 'OK!' he yelled. 'If Uncle's so lazy that he can go on a long ocean cruise, we won't bother telling him Aunt Kunnikunde is back and intends to destroy him! No, we won't!'

Hermann and Fritz looked at each other and frowned.

'Let's go, Rollover!' Farty abruptly turned to storm off but not before shouting an angry parting remark at the bemused plumber and painter: 'Don't forget, I'm a Count and a very important person!'

Neither Fritz nor Hermann were sure what they were supposed to do with that knowledge.

As Rollover followed Farty off the premises, he was staggered at his cousin's reaction. Here was a man, Rollover thought, who spent just one day in the office and then needed to take two weeks off for stress leave—and he was angry at Johann for taking a holiday? Nevertheless, Rollover was pleased by Farty's inadvertent warning about Kunnikunde, confident it would be passed on. All he had to do now was steel himself for a board meeting in three days, which he predicted his aunt would attend in person.

WIPE OUT

5

Back on the cruise ship, no steeling of oneself was necessary to cope with life in the lap of luxury, exquisite cuisine and exciting entertainment. The first two days passed quickly and before the passengers knew it, they had reached the harbour of Porto.

On disembarking, Johann and Andy were privileged to have their own private guide to show them around; Roger knew the port city extremely well.

After an enthralling day-long excursion, they returned to the *MS Teutonia* to see Michaela waving to them from the deck. She hadn't joined them on their walking tour, telling Andy that she needed to stay and prepare the ship against threat. 'What threat?' he had asked, but she had refused to say and simply walked away. Andy's initial annoyance at Michaela's tight-lipped response dissipated once he was being shown around the fascinating port city.

After returning Michaela's wave and moving along the dock platform to reboard the ship, Johann, Roger and Andy found their attention drawn to the sound of precision marching—the footsteps tapping out a rhythmic, military-like beat. As the sound got closer and louder, they could make out six men approaching the ship. All were dressed in black suits, white shirts and red ties, their gleaming boots perfectly matching their black helmets. Striding out front like an undersized bandleader without his baton was a pompous little man rubbing his hands together profusely.

'Folterknecht!' Roger groaned with a great sigh. 'This is not a good sign. Let's hope they don't join our ship; otherwise, Mrs Wurstling might be right, and we could be sinking after all!'

'Don't tell her that, for goodness' sake!' Johann gasped. 'I've already had to apologise to her for my earlier outburst!'

As they boarded the ship, Roger's hopes disintegrated when he saw Folterknecht and his henchmen also heading up the gangway.

The pompous little man didn't waste any time, immediately seeking out the ship's captain. 'I want access to your operating theatre to establish my laboratory! Yah!' he shouted at the top of his strident voice. 'I want no noise around my cabin . . . and one of the dining rooms is to be reserved exclusively for me and my men! Yah!'

'Negative! Negative! And negative, again, sir!' the captain shouted back with equal force.

'I am Dr Folterknecht!' the little man yelled, 'head of the Teutonian Secret Police! Yah! By that authority, I demand you yield to my command! Yah!'

'I'm the authority here!' thundered Captain Klump. 'I'm the commander on this ship! As such, I can decide that you have somehow booked yourselves onto the wrong vessel and will give you one minute to leave!'

Dr Folterknecht looked extremely angry, but the prospect of being thrown off the ship there and then calmed him down. 'In two or three days you will regret your hostile attitude, Captain, yah!' he hissed. With that, he turned on his heel and led his trained thugs away to locate their cabins.

Later that evening Johann, Roger, Andy and Michaela gathered in the bar, sharing a table with the Wurstlings. They had barely settled in before their conversation was cut short by Dr Folterknecht and his goons. They just waltzed right in as if they owned the place, barging their way between the tables without so much as a 'sorry' or a 'pardon me'.

'I demand a table, immediately!' Folterknecht bellowed at a waiter unfortunate enough to be close by.

'We are rather crowded, sir,' he said, 'but I will see—'

SLAP! The secret police chief's right hand connected with the poor waiter's face. 'Speak only when invited to do so, underling!' Folterknecht screeched.

The waiter stumbled off in a state of shock.

Unfortunately, the only table free with enough room for the doctor and his men was right in front of Johann's.

'Folterknecht!' shouted Commander Wurstling, upset at the doctor's treatment of the waiter. 'I'm watching you!'

'Wurstling!' a surprised Folterknecht barked. 'The bumbling police officer! You're still alive? Amazing! Last time I saw you, you were stuck in a cage with big cats! I guess you reeked so badly of incompetence they didn't want to risk eating you! Ha! Ha! Ha!'

'Even wild animals respect the authority of a Teutonian police officer!' Wurstling retorted.

At that moment Dr Folterknecht laid eyes on Roger, who met his gaze and raised his glass with a cheery smile.

'Roger Less!' the doctor screamed, jumping to his feet and somehow raising his voice even higher. 'A Britonnian spy on a Teutonian ship! I will shoot you! Yah! Burn you! Yah! Hang you! Yah! And then interrogate you! Yah!'

'Sit down! Stop this nonsense!' Captain Klump roared, suddenly appearing beside Folterknecht. 'You, sir!' he said, addressing the mad doctor, 'have been nothing but trouble since you first set foot on this ship! I'm considering throwing you off at our next stop in four days . . . unless you start behaving like a normal guest!'

Folterknecht sat down and started to giggle. 'Four days! Yah! A lot can happen in four days! Yah! Ha! Ha! Ha!' He continued laughing and his six colleagues joined in. Johann and his group chose that point to move from the bar to the restaurant, where they enjoyed a perfect dinner without the histrionics of the mad Dr Folterknecht.

Andy had never seen Michaela so relaxed and positive. It was a sign, he thought, that there would be no incidents on the immediate horizon. Perhaps his father had made the same assumption, Andy thought, because even he looked relaxed in Michaela's company. After dinner, the irresistible pleasures of the cigar lounge lured Johann and Roger away. Michaela and Andy preferred fresh air to cigar smoke and wandered off to stroll the decks in the glow of the moon that had turned the calm ocean a shimmering silver.

6

'THIS IS AN ACT OF PIRACY!' Captain Klump's voice thundered. 'WE ARE IN INTERNATIONAL WATERS!'

The sound of the captain's enraged voice booming through the loudspeakers at the front of the ship woke Andy with a jolt early in the morning just two days after his stroll in the moonlight with Michaela. He dressed in record time and rushed up on deck. The first thing he saw stopped him in his tracks. Directly ahead of the *MS Teutonia* were two massive warships blocking the way. Then Andy spotted Michaela observing it all from the bow of the cruise ship. Closer to the captain's bridge he saw Folterknecht and his henchmen standing to attention as if they were expecting someone important to arrive.

The mad doctor was rubbing his hands together profusely, looking positively excited. 'Those will be my ships!' he shouted at the bridge. 'You incompetent captain! Yah!'

Captain Klump couldn't have heard that up on the bridge; besides, he was fully engaged in trying to out-manoeuvre the warships.

Minutes later Andy was alarmed to see the warships each launch two patrol boats. The patrol boats began to circle the *MS Teutonia* at high speed, then two of the boats slowed down and drew alongside the cruise ship. Andy's alarm bordered on panic when he saw men on the patrol boats attaching devices to the ship's hull. He assumed the devices were explosives of some kind—probably limpet mines.

Andy was so tense he almost jumped out of his skin when he heard Michaela's voice in his head. 'I demagnetised our cruise ship,' she said, 'and made the limpet mines buoyant, which means that instead of sticking to our ship they will attach themselves to the warships! Enjoy my show!'

Looking closely, Andy could see the mines detaching from the cruise ship's hull and moving towards the two big warships. Meanwhile one of the warship's admirals was sending a loud and clear message to Captain Klump of the *MS Teutonia*: 'THIS IS THE GLORIOUS NAVY OF ROGANDA. STOP YOUR SHIP IMMEDIATELY. YOU HAVE BROKEN INTERNATIONAL MARITIME LAWS. WE WILL NEED TO BOARD YOU.'

By this time, of course, the passengers were all crowding the decks as terrified spectators to the unfolding drama.

As the announcement finished and echoed away across the water, the warships launched two large troop-carrier helicopters, which slowly approached the front of the cruise ship where Dr Folterknecht and his men were waiting. As the choppers hovered overhead, ropes were thrown onto the deck and Rogandan commandoes began to abseil down.

That was as far as they got. To the passengers' astonishment and disbelief, the whole terrifying spectacle disappeared in the blink of an eye. The helicopters, patrol boats and huge warships simply vanished. More correctly, however, it was the *MS Teutonia* that had disappeared. When Captain Klump checked his coordinates, he was surprised to discover that his ship was one hundred miles south of its original position, far away from the threat of the Rogandan navy.

Turning to his second-in-command, Chief Officer Fritz, Captain Klump demanded to be pinched, just in case this was all just a weird dream he was having.

'Yeeeowwww!' he screamed a second later, making everyone on the bridge jump. 'Fritz, you fool! Not so hard!'

'Sorry, Captain!'

'Well, at least I know I'm not dreaming,' Klump muttered, rubbing his arm. Then he did something smart. He ordered a complete lockdown of the bridge and set the *MS Teutonia* on course full steam ahead towards their next stop, the island of Madusa.

The Rogandan Navy, meanwhile, was in total disarray. Helicopters swirled around with commandoes hanging from ropes with nowhere to land, except in the ocean, which most eventually did. Patrol boats zoomed pointlessly in all directions while the admirals of the two big warships were too stunned and confused to issue any orders. Chaos reigned. Finally, the radar and radio operators picked up Dr Folterknecht's radio beacon, which they had been relying on, and fixed it at a point one hundred miles due south.

By now the two Rogandan admirals had composed themselves somewhat and started communicating by radio from their respective bridges. One of them suggested activating the mines they had attached to the cruise ship. 'That will sink the cruise ship and then when we reach its position in about six hours, we can at least pick up some hostages.'

'Yes! Let's do it!'

A minute later, the admirals simultaneously pushed red buttons on their control panels. The last thing either of them expected to hear was the sound of two massive explosions. The force threw them both to the floor, along with everyone else aboard the warships. By the time they dragged themselves to their feet, all thoughts of the *MS Teutonia* evaporated. The admirals' only concern now was the gaping holes in their warships; the battle to keep the pride of the Rogandan Navy afloat had begun.

7

On board the *MS Teutonia*, Andy was keeping a keen eye on Dr Folterknecht and his men as they frantically scanned the ocean with their binoculars for signs of the Rogandan warships. The mad doctor had worked himself into a state of bewildered hysteria. 'What happened? What happened? Yah! Yah!' he continuously cried out, running all about the deck for different vantage points, his men right behind him. He eventually stopped asking what happened and just kept yelling 'Yah! Yah!' non-stop. He finally gave up and slumped in a deck chair, exhausted.

Just then, Michaela casually walked past and Folterknecht managed to rally himself enough to bail her up.

'Young lady!' he demanded. 'Did you see what happened? Yah! Did you see?'

'Sorry, sir,' Michaela smiled at him. 'I was meditating.'

'Meditating?'

'Yes, sir. While I'm meditating, I see nothing.'

'Aaarrrrgh!' Folterknecht snarled. He waited till Michaela had moved on and then said to his men, 'Since we can't count on our Rogandan friends, we'll have to take over this ship ourselves! Collect your assault weapons and come to my cabin in precisely one hour. Yah!'

At that moment, the captain's voice rang out through the intercom: 'THE PIRATE WARSHIPS WISELY DECIDED NOT TO ATTACK US AND EVERYTHING IS BACK TO NORMAL. IN FACT, WE ARE AHEAD OF SCHEDULE AND WILL REACH THE ISLAND OF MADUSA TOMORROW AFTERNOON . . . SEVEN HOURS EARLIER THAN PLANNED. THANK YOU.'

'The incompetent Captain Klump!' Folterknecht sneered. 'After we meet in my cabin, we will take over his bridge! Yah!'

About an hour later Andy met his father, Roger and Michaela for breakfast in the main restaurant. Both men had been asleep during the warship crisis and knew nothing of what had gone down.

As they selected their buffet breakfasts, Roger was the first to notice one of Folterknecht's men positioning himself at the restaurant entrance. Wearing a helmet and a long black coat he stood out like a fish in a tree among the colourfully-dressed holidaymakers.

'That's one of Folterknecht's men,' Roger said, pointing him out to the others. 'What's he up to? I'll think I'll go and check him out.'

He started to get up from his chair but was stopped short by a vehement 'No!' from Michaela and sat back down again.

'Both of you,' she ordered, 'enjoy your holiday and don't involve yourselves in minor incidents that I can handle quite easily!'

Roger and Johann looked at one another and shrugged, then got back to their breakfasts.

Things did not go well for Dr Folterknecht and his plans. After he had placed four of his men equipped with assault rifles at strategic points throughout the ship, he tried to enter the captain's bridge with his other two men. They men attempted to smash the doors in but to no avail; the doors were sturdily reinforced and bullet proof. Captain Klump's earlier decision to lock down the bridge had proved to be a perceptive one indeed.

Thwarted at his very first step in taking over the ship, Folterknecht became enraged. 'I will eliminate one passenger after another until you change your course towards Roganda! Yah!' he screamed at the locked door. 'The fate of your passengers is in your hands! Yah! You have one minute to decide! Yah!'

On the other side of the door, Captain Klump decided he must be having another weird dream. Michaela had just appeared right beside him . . . in his locked-down bridge! 'Pinch me again, Fritz!'

Fritz obliged.

'Yeeeowwww!' Klump screeched. 'Not so hard, Fritz . . . for goodness' sake!'

'Captain!' Michaela interjected. 'Hold your course! Your passengers will be safe!' With that, she disappeared.

'What was that?' Klump gasped.

'It was an angel, sir!' Fritz explained.

Whatever it was, Captain Klump decided to put his faith in it. Bluffing, he shouted at the bolted door to Folterknecht, 'I don't care about the passengers! I only care about my ship!'

Dr Folterknecht was completely taken aback. His instinctive response to threaten people with physical violence as a negotiating tool had never been given such short shrift. He was momentarily impressed with the captain's remark. He should be working for me! Yah! he told himself. He has the perfect attitude! Yah! But the doctor's insanity quickly reasserted itself and he decided that executing passengers in view of the bridge would eventually convince the captain to change course. He and his two men threw off their big coats and, with guns drawn, rushed towards the stairs that led to the main deck.

8

As the mad doctor and his men rattled down the metal steps, none of them noticed Michaela standing at the bottom watching them with an amused smile. Folterknecht was the first to lose his footing. He fell down the steps and landed flat on his face on the deck. His two colleagues followed, piling right on top of him.

'Get off me! Get off me, you clumsy oafs! Yah!' screeched the mad doctor.

Dragging themselves to their feet, moaning and groaning, they were startled to see Michaela standing before them with one of their guns in her hand.

'Nice gun,' she said with a sweet smile. 'Are they legal on this ship?'

'Lady!' Folterknecht yelled angrily, his nose streaming blood. 'Hand over the gun! Yah!' He lunged at Michaela and grabbed the gun from her hand. The weapon was suddenly a hundred times heavier than normal. It was as if Michaela had handed Folterknecht an anvil. He was jolted violently backwards, crashing onto the deck once again. The weight of the anvil gun broke several of his fingers, and probably some ribs as well. He howled in pain. He howled even louder when Michaela wrenched the gun from his hand and threw it into the sea.

'Only grown men should be allowed to carry guns,' Michaela scolded. She repeated the process with the other two men and threw their guns into the sea as well.

Andy, who had heard the commotion, came running, arriving just in time to see the guns sailing over the railing. Before they hit the water they evaporated into thin air.

'Who are you?' screamed the badly hurt Folterknecht.

'I'm just your everyday alien, sir,' Michaela teased.

'I knew it! Yah! I knew it!' squealed the doctor. 'I will catch you! Yah! I will dissect you! Yah!' He continued to squeal a litany of barbarous threats as the ship's security officer handcuffed him and his two men and led them away to the brig.

Observing the mad doctor's demise, Captain Klump reopened the bridge. Michaela commandeered the intercom and, imitating Folterknecht's voice perfectly, announced, 'All in order! Yah! Mission accomplished! Yah! Everyone back to your rooms and dismantle your weapons! Yah!' Folterknecht's men were totally fooled and followed the command without question.

That evening at dinner, Captain Klump joined Johann's table and hit it off well with Commander Wurstling, although he seemed somewhat offended by Mrs Wurstling's life-saving attire.

Back in Stone, Rollover von Cracklingen's prediction that his Aunt Kunnikunde would suddenly appear in person at their board meeting proved to be correct.

'I'm only here for a short time!' she announced to the barely concealed relief of her three directors. 'I have to do a job the devil himself could not do!' An evil smile spread over her face as she turned to Rollover. 'Drive me to Johann's place, nephew! I have a meeting with him . . . a final meeting!' She giggled loudly with delight as she started to march from the room, waving Rollover to follow her.

'But Aunt, Johann is not—'

'Shush, Rollover!' Kunnikunde hissed. 'Not another word out of you! I have to focus!'

A small dot, like a tiny black ball, appeared above his aunt's head, which Rollover tried to ignore. He simply shook his head and did as he was told. When he pulled Kunnikunde's limousine up at Johann's place, she jumped out and took a big breath. Instantly the tiny ball above her head expanded into a mini swirling thunderstorm cloud.

She really is a witch! Rollover told himself with shock and horror as his evil aunt headed towards the front door. Before she reached it, the door opened to reveal Hermann and Fritz blocking the way.

'Out of the way, peasants!' Kunnikunde shrieked as she pushed her way past them into the house. She rushed from one room to the next without finding anyone. 'Find them!' she ordered her tame storm cloud, which zoomed from room to room unhindered by walls. Kunnikunde sat in a lounge chair, calling out in her sweetest voice, 'Johann! Anna! Andy! Please come into the living room . . . I have a surprise for you!'

'They're not here,' gasped a nervous Fritz. 'They're on holiday!'

'What? What? Holidays? How can they afford that? Johann never takes holidays! Why wasn't I informed?'

When her storm cloud returned, it confirmed the family's absence and reminded her that she could still set up the devil's trap for them upon their return.

'Get out! Get out!' Kunnikunde screeched at Hermann and Fritz. 'I need some time alone!'

When the storm cloud started threatening the men, the two house-sitters had no choice but to leave the house. Kunnikunde, smiling happily, then placed the devil's marbles carefully around the living room before she too left the house. Outside, her attitude to Hermann and Fritz changed completely. Ever so politely, she enquired sweetly as to when the family was expected to return. Getting an approximate date, she gestured to Rollover, and they left.

'You knew it!' Kunnikunde hissed at Rollover on their drive back to the company offices! 'You knew they were gone and didn't tell me!'

'I tried to tell you, Aunt . . . but you shushed me.'

Kunnikunde was about to abuse him again when the cloud above her head intervened and calmed her down. It told her that the visit to Johann's was a success. How else, it said, could she have set the trap? Everything was now ready for the elimination of Count Johann Ritter von Krumm and his family. This instantly changed Kunnikunde's mood for the better.

Back in the boardroom, Kunnikunde made it clear to her directors that their only priority from that moment on was to spy on Johann and his family and let her know in advance exactly when they would return from their holidays.

'I will hit them the instant they get home, before they settle in! Ha! Ha! Ha!' With that, she disappeared into thin air.

9

At that moment a long way away, Dr Folterknecht was wishing he could disappear into thin air too. Instead, he and his six henchmen had to settle for being unceremoniously escorted off the ship in handcuffs when the *MS Teutonia* docked at Medusa Island harbour.

'This is sabotage!' Folterknecht shouted at Captain Klump. 'I will be back for the alien! Yah! And I will see you in court! Yah! For harassment and bullying! Yah!' When the doctor realised that the luggage leaving the ship with him contained only clothing and no equipment or weapons, he lost it completely, nearly fainting with rage.

Roger, Michaela, and Andy inspected Folterknecht's arsenal. They were astonished and horrified at his array of tools for destruction. Roger identified many of the weapons, while Michaela focused on the various chemicals. 'If these substances were to fall back into the wrong hands,' she declared, 'the results could be catastrophic. Some of them could be used for chemical warfare.' She held up three vials of red liquid. 'And these are filled with viruses that could wipe out a whole city!'

'No wonder the Rogandans were so keen to do business with Folterknecht,' Roger said. 'The man's a homicidal maniac!'

'How can we destroy the chemicals?' Andy asked.

'I have already,' Michaela responded. 'I have rendered them inert. These vials are now full of harmless liquid, and I want them returned to the mad doctor. We need to follow their trail. We must find out what he's up to and exactly who he plans to give the chemicals to.'

'I'm sure that will be Ido Farkheem, the brutal, megalomaniac dictator of Roganda,' Roger declared. 'He is always trying to procure deadly weapons and sometimes even uses them on his own people in order to stay in power.'

'That would make him an attractive ally for Folterknecht,' Michaela remarked.

'Monstrous lunatics attract,' Roger said.

It took the three of them a little while to convince Captain Klump to hand Folterknecht's chemicals back to the mad doctor, but since the seized guns were staying on board, he reluctantly agreed.

When Dr Folterknecht regained possession of his cache of evil chemicals his fury abated. He triumphantly announced to his men that they were back in business. Holding up the three vials of red liquid he cried out, 'Just two drops of this would turn the *MS Teutonia* into a ghost ship! Yah! I will take my revenge! Yah! But first, let's book a flight to Roganda! Yah! I have a very important meeting there with the president! Yah!'

With the mad doctor gone and his arsenal of chemicals rendered harmless, everyone had a fantastic holiday on Madusa, swimming, sailing and cycling . . . and of course eating and drinking aplenty. Michaela reverted to her spirit form and returned to the magic pencil for a rest. After nearly three days on the island, the ship set sail for Kinkanza on the last leg of its cruise. It was also the final destination for Andy, where he would participate in the nature park expedition.

Disembarking in Calisburg, the capital of Kinkanza, provided a new experience for Andy; it was the first time in his life that he had been in a city full of skyscrapers. He had barely had a quick look around before Johann and Roger dropped him off at the train that would take him to the expedition campsite to meet his fellow students and Professor Katz-Kopf. Johann and Roger also parted ways; Johann headed off to investigate local forestry and plantation methods, and Roger went on to his undercover mission on behalf of Her Majesty of Britonnia's Secret Service.

After a long train ride, Andy was greeted by a park ranger, who would drive him to the campsite. 'Welcome, Andy,' the ranger said. 'My name is Rory. We should have an interesting drive; we will be travelling on dirt roads through some natural bushland and should see plenty of wildlife.'

He wasn't wrong. Partway into their journey, they encountered a large herd of elephants resting on a section of the dirt road. All traffic was blocked. When a big bull elephant took a threatening stance towards their four-wheel-drive vehicle, Ranger Rory was on instant alert. Andy, on the other hand, was relaxed, completely in awe at seeing these beautiful animals.

'Quiet as a mouse!' Ranger Rory whispered to Andy. 'Don't move! We call this bull "Igor the Terrible" because of his aggressiveness.'

After half an hour there was still no sign the mighty animals were going to move on. 'Do you have any food for them in the car?' Andy whispered.

'Yes,' Rory replied. 'In the back, there's a bag of bark chips, their favourite food—but it weighs nearly a hundred kilograms. And anyway, even if you tried to feed them, Igor would trample you before you could give him a single chip.'

'Not me!' Andy said jauntily, leaping out of the car and grabbing the bag of bark chips from the back of the vehicle. He threw the bag over his shoulder as if it were a sock full of feathers and started to stroll towards Igor the Terrible.

The park ranger gasped in horror. 'What? Come back, you idiot!' he yelled, deciding whispering was no longer practical. 'He'll crush you like a bug!'

Igor raised his trunk and began flapping his ears as Andy approached. Then letting loose a blaring trumpeting sound, the massive elephant charged right at him.

Andy calmly raised one hand and called out, 'STOP, old fellow!'

Igor stopped just a few feet short, throwing up a small cloud of dust that settled over Andy. Andy, coughing, set down the bag of bark chips and ripped it open. Igor helped himself, virtually ignoring his benefactor, while the ranger, still in his vehicle, sat in stunned disbelief. Emptying a quantity of the chips onto the ground for Igor, Andy carried the bag over to the herd and used it to lure them into the field beside the road. Once there he spread the bark chips all around and the elephants stayed in the field eating them. Two baby elephants followed Andy around until he left the field and returned to the vehicle. Ranger Rory was speechless. He stared at Andy in disbelief, shaking his head as they drove off.

About twenty minutes before they reached the campsite, the ranger finally regained his power of speech. 'A one-hundred-kilogram bag you lifted as if it were empty! How is that possible? You don't look that strong! And huge aggressive wild animals following you as if they were your pets! Tell me I was dreaming, young man!

'Oh, you just have to know the right way to sling a heavy bag over your shoulder,' Andy said. 'And animals just seem to like me—I can't explain it.'

This seemed to mollify the ranger somewhat. After staring at Andy again for a time and shaking his head some more, Rory continued on the rest of the journey in silence.

10

'Dolittle! Welcome to the adventure of your lifetime!' Professor Katz-Kopf proclaimed exuberantly as Andy and the ranger pulled up at the campsite. He was clearly happy to see his star student.

'We've already had the adventure of my lifetime!' Ranger Rory blurted out, his voice suddenly returning once again. 'He turned wild elephants into his pets!'

'Oh yes, that fits!' nodded the professor. 'That's my Dolittle!'

After greeting his fellow students, Andy proceeded to find his accommodation. The camp consisted of about twenty-five compact cabins surrounding the main building. When he located his cabin and went inside, Andy was surprised to find it very clean and comfortable; he hadn't expected to have all the amenities he could possibly want in a simple campground. He continued to be impressed when he checked out the restaurant in the main building; it looked relaxing and inviting and had a large wood-fired barbecue.

That evening, the students, rangers and professor gathered round the barbecue cooking their own steaks and discussing their plans for the upcoming week. Andy noticed the presence of quite a few soldiers.

'They are our anti-poaching squad,' the ranger explained. 'They try to prevent the illegal killing of the park's animals.'

'Where do these poachers come from?' Andy asked. 'Are they local?'

'No,' Ranger Rory replied vehemently. 'Our people value the wild animals. The poachers invade us from Roganda—the border is just five kilometres away—and very recently the poachers became well-equipped and organised, posing an even greater threat to the animals. We need a lot more soldiers as reinforcements, but so far, the government has denied our requests, saying it is too expensive.'

Andy's mind was working overtime. He asked Rory to introduce him to a couple of the soldiers. After asking them a few questions, Andy said, 'I would love to come on one of your patrols. Could that be arranged?'

The soldiers just stared at him as if he were crazy then burst into uproarious laughter. At that point, Ranger Rory stepped in and told them about Andy's extraordinary handling of the wild elephants. The soldiers were mightily impressed and changed their mindset, agreeing to take Andy on a patrol provided he sign official liability waivers indicating he would be accompanying the patrol at his own risk.

The next morning, ensuring he had the magic pencil securely buttoned inside his shirt pocket, Andy joined the soldiers on what would be an all-day exercise patrolling the Kinkanza–Roganda border areas. Their convoy of four camouflaged military-Jeep-like vehicles passed through both open savanna and thick forest, providing Andy with amazing views of many different kinds of wild animals. He was fascinated and delighted to see lions, antelopes, giraffes, zebras, elephants, and even several rhinoceroses.

About two hours into their patrol, they heard fierce growling and snarling coming from a thicket a little way off the track. Approaching extremely carefully, they discovered a distressed lioness with her hind leg caught in a powerful steel trap. She was accompanied by two crying cubs: one an adolescent and the other still very young, both just circling helplessly around their mother.

The lioness was near exhaustion from her frantic struggles, lying on her stomach but still trying to free herself.

Andy was grateful that Professor Katz-Kopf had loaned him his medical bag. He grabbed it and moved towards the lioness.

'Stop!' shouted the patrol commander. 'That trap takes four men to open—and even if you manage it, the lioness will tear you apart!'

Too late. Andy had already reached the awful scene and was greeted with great enthusiasm by the two cubs. With his super strength, Andy had no trouble removing the trap from the lioness's leg. For good measure, he angrily crushed the trap into a ball of twisted steel so it could never be used again.

The lioness, released from the trap, painfully dragged herself to her feet and, to the astonishment of the soldiers, allowed Andy to treat her lacerated leg. Andy was relieved to find there were no broken bones and proceeded to clean the wounds on each side of the animal's leg. He shaved parts of her fur away and stitched up the gaping gashes and puncture holes. He then applied a disinfectant and dressed the wounds.

Andy took a minute to say goodbye to the two cubs as their mother pushed her way in and licked Andy on the face. For the patrol commander and his soldiers, what they were witnessing was beyond belief. Their reaction was a blend of wonder, fear and bewilderment.

Back in the Jeep, Andy connected by telepathy with the magic pencil, wanting to know if there were any more traps in the vicinity.

'Yes, Andy,' came the reply, 'there are six more.'

Clear images of the whereabouts of those traps instantly appeared in Andy's head. The commander, who was now staring at Andy as if he were a ghost, or a sorcerer, willingly followed his directions. They located the traps in quick succession, and Andy set each one off with a sharp punch that was so fast he wasn't hurt.

'Impossible!' cried the commander. 'Physically impossible!' He then told himself nothing was impossible with this incredible young man. While the commander wrestled with his grip on reality, Andy destroyed each of the six traps the same way he had the first one.

Despite their lingering state of shock and disbelief, the anti-poaching squad members were extremely happy with their results so far; never before had they uncovered so many traps so quickly and efficiently.

As they continued their patrol the magic pencil alerted Andy that a large gang of poachers armed with high-powered rifles was crossing the border into the national park. 'Looks more like a small army to me,' the pencil said. 'Thirty-two of them with a supply truck and two armoured vehicles . . . waiting in ambush for you.'

Several minutes later, the patrol commander barked out an order: 'We'll set up our base camp here.'

At that moment, Andy heard a sound that took him back to a scary encounter years before with his dog Sassy in a cornfield on the outskirts of Stone. 'It's a drone!' he cried, scanning the sky.

11

When Andy pointed at the drone overhead, the patrol commander got off two quick shots right on target, bringing the tiny craft crashing to the ground.

'Well done!' Andy called out, applauding enthusiastically. 'Brilliant shooting!'

The commander beamed at Andy and stuck his thumb up. Leaping out of his Jeep and with Andy close behind, he rushed over to the crashed drone. 'Very unusual,' the commander said, scowling. 'Not a good sign. Previously the poachers lacked such sophistication! And worse still, this is a Rogandan Army drone!'

'Yes, it is the Rogandan Army's, and they are up to no good!'

The female voice in the Jeep right behind the commander made him jump. He swung round to see Michaela smiling at him.

'What? Where did you come from?' he yelled out. 'Who let this lady join our patrol?'

'That would have been me,' Andy announced. 'And I'm so glad she is here.'

'A society lady dressed up as Wonder Woman is the last thing we need on our patrol!' the commander shouted. The words were barely out of his mouth when Michaela zapped a second drone out of the air. She touched its camera and threw it back towards the rapidly approaching Rogandan soldiers. It was such a mighty throw that the patrol commander was rendered speechless with shock once again.

'Not a society lady!' Michaela smiled at him, unable to resist teasing him. Suddenly she was all business: 'Andy! Stay here and protect the patrol! I'll send you my coordinates when I need you!' At that, she disappeared into thin air.

The commander suffered an instant anxiety attack. 'Someone kick me! Someone kick me! I'm dreaming! He cried. 'And please kick me hard!'

There was no lack of volunteers at such an irresistible invitation. The soldiers had never before been given the opportunity to kick their commanding officer with impunity. The commander's own driver was the first to take up the offer, delivering a mighty kick to his boss's shin. The victim yelled out in pain. 'Not so hard, you fool!'

As he doubled over rubbing his shin, a second soldier landed a massive kick on his backside, sending him sprawling on his face in the dust. 'Enough!' he shouted. 'The invitation is withdrawn!'

Several of the other soldiers looked bitterly disappointed at this. The commander hobbled back to his Jeep and collapsed into his seat, his meltdown continuing. 'Why can't I wake up!' he lamented.

Making matters worse for the commander, Andy, having received Michaela's coordinates, also vanished right in front of the commander's eyes.

Andy landed beside Michaela a short distance away from the intruding Rogandan soldiers. They watched them closely for several minutes, observing a great deal of activity around one of their vehicles.

'They are attaching a tiny parcel to one of their drones. I will need to find out what it is,' Michaela explained before disappearing. 'Oh, oh!' she said upon her return seconds later. 'Just as I suspected! Dr Folterknecht's weapon of mass destruction has found its way to the Rogandan Army! It's a vial of his deadly virus—or what used to be a deadly virus before I deactivated it on the ship. If it still had its evil properties, it could have wiped out most of the animals in the park, including any humans. Dastardly indeed!'

'These people are vile barbarians!' Andy exclaimed furiously. 'So how do we deal with them?'

'Wait until they launch their drone with their impotent 'deadly virus' and then we will scare them back to Roganda!' Michaela said with a laugh.

When their drone took off with its 'deadly' payload, the Rogandan soldiers all cheered then went back to work digging a long, deep trench big enough to hide most of the soldiers. Their simple plan was to send two soldiers, dressed as poachers, in a Jeep out towards the anti-poaching squad and then lure the anti-poachers back to where the soldiers lay in ambush in the trench.

Michaela's three-stage retaliatory plan was even simpler: First, disarm the soldiers in the trench. Second, disable their armoured vehicles. Third, capture their supply truck undamaged. The truck's collection of equipment, weapons and ammunition would turn the anti-poaching squad into a formidable protective unit—something their head office in Calisburg had so far failed to do.

'Shall I teleport myself into the supply truck and drive it out?' Andy suggested.

'No!' Michaela retorted. 'Just grab it!'

'What?' Andy cried, but Michaela was gone.

It took her less than a second to disarm thirty-two soldiers, and when Andy reached the scene, they had all disappeared.

'Where are they?' Andy stammered.

'Grab the truck, Andy . . . to your right!' Michaela scolded.

'What? Oh, yes!' Andy said, seeing the supply truck was now toy size and would sit easily in the palm of his hand. He noticed Michaela had also shrunk the Rogandan soldiers to the size of insects. Still in their trenches, the walls were now huge cliffs. The soldiers were fighting off numerous ants, which were now as big as they were, and ten times stronger.

'They'll return to their original size,' Michaela said, smiling, 'but not for hours.'

Michaela touched Andy and they were both instantly teleported to within a kilometre of the anti-poaching patrol. At that precise moment, the toy-size supply truck in Andy's hand reverted to life-size and he found himself pinned underneath it. He was easily able to lift it and get out without injury, except for a bruised ego.

'Very funny!' he grumbled.

'A good test!' laughed Michaela. 'Your shield is still working perfectly.'

She placed the confiscated weapons into the truck and drove it towards the patrol with Andy running along in front.

Not far ahead of them, also racing towards the anti-poaching patrol, was the Rogandan Jeep with the two pretend poachers who were attempting to lure the patrol back to the trench trap. Just before the Jeep reached the patrol's base it did a spectacular U-turn in a massive cloud of dust and dirt and then raced back the way it had come. It certainly caught the attention of the anti-poaching patrol commander and soldiers, who immediately gave chase.

The Rogandan Jeep flashed past Andy and Michaela, followed seconds later by the anti-poaching squad Jeeps in hot pursuit.

'Faster! Faster!' yelled the commander, ignoring Andy and Michaela in the supply truck racing past them in the opposite direction.

'They would have driven straight into the trap!' Andy cried. 'If you hadn't shrunk the Rogandan soldiers, the entire anti-poaching patrol would have been ambushed.'

Following orders, the two Rogandan pretend poachers drove the Jeep past the hidden trenches, then stopped and got out with their hands in the air. The anti-poaching patrol Jeeps roared to a halt on either side of them. This should have been the moment for the Rogandan troops in the trenches to open fire. The two

Rogandans looked at each other in bewilderment, then started yelling, 'Hello! Hello? We're here!'

'I know where you are, monkey brains!' shouted the anti-poaching patrol commander. 'I can see you! You're under arrest! Handcuff them!'

'Don't shoot! Don't shoot!' the captives cried all the way back to the vehicle, expecting their fellow soldiers to start firing from the trenches.

'Don't tempt me!' the commander shouted and gave the order to head back to the base.

12

By the time the patrol got back to base camp, Michaela had returned to the magic pencil and Andy was alone with the captured supply truck. The amazed patrol became very excited when they saw it. Inside they found not only guns and ammunition but also the latest in night vision goggles, bullet proof vests and other useful equipment.

'How did—' the commander started to say then stopped himself. He was also going to ask what had become of Wonder Woman but decided against that too. 'Better I don't ask,' he muttered.

His anti-poaching soldiers weren't asking any questions either, but they were bursting with stories of the day's incredible events in the bush.

Of course, there was one massive story the anti-poaching unit knew nothing about. Over the mountain, not far from where they had encountered the Rogandan drones, lay an enormous military base with airstrips, fighter planes in specially built bunkers, missile launchers, tanks, armoured vehicles and thousands of soldiers. Also integrated into the base were three native villages. And overlooking it all was a palatial building set into the side of the mountain itself.

This extravagant facility was the military headquarters of the brutal dictator Ido Farkheem. His political head office and main seat of power was his palace in Roganda's capital city, Lebola. Several hours from the capital was another huge complex, which was rumoured to house advanced laboratories dedicated to the development of chemical and viral weapons of mass destruction. No surprise, then, that the occupants of a small bus arriving at the palace turned out to be Dr Folterknecht and his henchmen.

The men stepped off the bus and eagerly marched inside, the doctor rubbing his hands together profusely. There they were met by Dictator Farkheem's head of chemical weapons research, Dr Idi Amonia.

'Idi! Yah!' exclaimed Folterknecht with delight. 'Your boss Ido has told me great things about your laboratory! Yah! I want to inspect it immediately! Yah! I especially need to inspect your control room to make sure my little device is set correctly. It is designed to eliminate the animals of Kinkanza Nature Park. Yah! . . . So, it must be calibrated with perfect precision! Yah!'

Both men then seemed to compete to see who had the eviler grin. They smirked and leered at one another for several seconds like demented chimpanzees, with no clear winner being declared.

Arriving at the laboratory, the mad doctor was amazed by what he saw. The lab was not only huge but equipped with state-of-the-art technology. All around him were at least a hundred men and women in white coats and safety glasses busy at their stainless-steel benches weighing, measuring and testing numerous substances of every colour and consistency. 'Yah!' Folterknecht exclaimed, feeling right at home. After being assigned a large office, he rushed back into the laboratory to collect the supply of evil chemicals he had brought with him from Teutonia. Idi Amonia was hot on his heels.

'Stop! Halt! *Achtung!*' the doctor screeched upon reaching his room to find a man in a white coat rummaging through his luggage. 'Yah! What are you doing? Stop!'

Idi Amonia, witnessing the intrusion, pressed a red button on a small device he carried in his pocket. Instantly four guards appeared and attempted to arrest the intruder.

Whack! Whack! Kick! Kick! In the blink of an eye, the four guards were lying on the floor. The same fate befell the next four guards to appear, and the four after that, and so on. Twenty-eight guards were quickly dispatched by the man in the white coat before multiple tasers were brought to bear and the man finally succumbed.

'Bring this criminal to my office!' shrieked Dr Folterknecht, incandescent with rage.

When they dragged the intruder, now handcuffed, to the doctor's office, Folterknecht's face changed from rage to astonishment and then to utmost delight. 'Ha! Ha! Ha! Yah!' he shrieked crazily. 'What do we have here? Yah! A Britonnian spy no less! How wonderful to see you again . . . Mr Roger Less! Yah! What a marvellous surprise! Yah!'

'No surprise to me, devil doctor,' Roger retorted with a cheery smile.

'Throw him in jail!' Folterknecht yelled. He glanced at Dr Amonia. 'I trust you have one, Idi?'

'This facility has a jail that can hold thousands,' Amonia boasted, 'with cutting edge torture chambers, so to speak, which our great leader President Farkheem loves to operate!'

'Excellent! Yah!' Folterknecht cried, rubbing his hands together profusely. He watched happily as Roger was dragged to an elevator that led straight to the jail complex. 'We have work to do!' Folterknecht barked, turning to his henchmen. 'President Farkheem is arriving tomorrow! Yah! Together we have some conquering to do—first Kinkanza and then the world! Yah! Ha! Ha! Ha!'

The henchmen were kept busy the rest of the day setting up what the mad doctor thought were deadly weapons of mass destruction, unaware that the magic pencil had rendered them useless.

Roger was thrown into a sparse cell and told that his old friend Dr Folterknecht would visit him and personally introduce him to President Farkheem.

'I have the sense that our friend Roger is in deep trouble,' the pencil's voice in Andy's head declared. 'I must check it out.'

'Can I join you?' Andy asked, but the pencil spirit had gone.

In his cell, Roger started to think long and hard about a way to escape. Fortunately, they had left him with his wristwatch, which with its high-powered, built-in laser capacity could easily cut a hole in his cell door. But then he would still have to contend with at least fifty guards. He deeply regretted leaving behind his supply of tiny personal attack drones. With them in hand he could have certainly taken out thirty guards, giving himself a real chance of escape.

Roger suddenly heard a familiar scolding voice ringing out in his head. 'Yes! Of course, hindsight is a wonderful thing! But what is much better is proper thinking at the beginning. Especially when you single-handedly try to take on the most heavily fortified facility in the world! It's P6, Mr Less—Prior Planning and Preparation Prevents Poor Performance!'

'Oh!' Roger exclaimed in his thoughts. 'For the first time I'm glad to hear from you . . . even if you are berating me!'

'Now listen carefully!' the pencil demanded with its usual brusqueness. 'There's a small pebble next to you. Grab it now and then when I say go, you drop it. Understood?'

Roger picked up the pebble. 'Ready when you are!' he said.

'Go!' the pencil's voice in his head commanded.

Roger dropped the pebble and ZAP! He instantly found himself in Andy's cabin at the Kinkanza Nature Park campsite.

'Welcome!' Andy managed to gasp, astonished to see him.

'Actually, I had it all under control,' Roger declared unconvincingly.

'Sure, you did!' retorted Michaela dryly as she rematerialised beside him.'

'Did you replicate me again?' Roger asked.

'No, not exactly,' Michaela replied. 'I left a robot version of you in the cell. It can only whack and kick and laugh, without feelings, and keep on doing it.'

'Well, that's pretty stupid!' Roger said.

'Yes,' Michaela said with a big smile, 'it's an exact copy of the original.'

'Ho! Ho!' retorted Roger. 'Very funny . . . not!'

'In exactly nine hours,' Michaela said, 'the president of Roganda will arrive at the laboratory. I have linked myself to their security system, which will allow us to listen in and learn what they're plotting to do. We must stay focused! Get some sleep—you need to be rested and sharp tomorrow.' With that, Michaela returned as a spirit into the magic pencil.

Andy and Roger had dinner at the restaurant and chatted for several hours before finally saying good night and going to bed.

13

The next day, Dr Folterknecht couldn't wait to interrogate his old foe Roger Less, the Britonnian secret agent. He had his office especially prepared, having his goons neatly lay out an array of injections, exotic drips and some old-fashioned torture tools for good measure. Once he was satisfied that everything was in readiness, he clapped his hands and yelped with joy. 'Yah! He will talk and tell me everything! Yah! Bring the prisoner here! Yah!' he ordered.

Shortly afterwards a happy-looking fake Roger was carried into the room in handcuffs with his legs chained together.

'What a wonderful day, yah, Sir Roger!' chirped the mad doctor. 'Finally, we can have a long meeting where we can exchange our deep knowledge of secret policing! Yah!' He raised his voice a little. 'And we want you to share every move and detail of your ugly queen! Yah! And I want to know everything you know about Britonnia and its strengths and weaknesses! Yah! I have ways and means of making you talk! Yah!'

The fake Roger just stood there smiling happily. Folterknecht ordered his goons to secure him in a special chair.

'What is your name, rank and identity? Yah!'

'Ha! Ha! Heh! Heh! Hi! Hi!' was the only response the doctor got.

'Aaarrrrgh!' screeched the doctor. 'You Britonnian agents are so smug! Yah! Soooo funnnnny! Yah! But stupid . . . very stupid! Yah!' He rushed to his table and grabbed a syringe full of bright yellow liquid. 'I will now inject you with a truth serum! Yah! That also will take care of your sense of humour! Yah!' Without delay, he plunged the needle deep into his victim's thigh. 'Perfect! Yah! Now we will wait for five minutes and then have a nice little chat! Yah!'

The fake Roger looked unperturbed and kept on smiling.

At that moment, Dr Idi Amonia rushed in and whispered in Folterknecht's ear.

'Oh! Oh! We are ready! Yah!' the mad doctor yelped. 'Take the prisoner into the grand hall; my friend President Ido is here!'

Suddenly the whole place was a hive of frantic activity—cleaners doing a last buff and shine and scientists ensuring their workstations were spick and span, while heavily armed soldiers tramped through the corridors towards the grand hall. Happily grinning, fake Roger was dragged in the same direction. Once in the hall, he was placed in the centre of the front row facing a row of twelve empty chairs set on either side of a very large golden throne-like chair.

The hall filled quickly with hundreds of people, surrounded by almost as many armed guards. The sound of a marching band grew steadily louder as it approached with the brutal dictator President Ido Farkheem following behind, making a grand entrance full of pomp and splendour. The president was a big man with an ugly face that seemed to be struck by perpetual anger . . . and perhaps a truck or two sometime in the past. Once the band stopped playing, President Farkheem took his seat. To his right sat Dr Idi Amonia and other scientists and to his left, two army generals and several ministers. Farkheem somehow added a look of utter boredom to his permanently angry expression, demanding to see Folterknecht's prisoner.

'Yes, Your Magnificence! Yah!' the mad doctor yelled out. 'Allow me to introduce the famous Britonnian spy, Mr Roger Less!'

The prisoner was pushed forward right in front of the dictator and stood gazing at him with a happy smile.

'Uncuff him and remover his chains!' Farkheem snapped. 'We have enough guards here to foil any escape attempt.'

The mad doctor stood up and approached the prisoner. 'I have injected this treacherous spy with a dose of my latest truth serum! Yah!' he announced. 'He will tell the truth, nothing but the truth! Yah!'

The president's look of boredom lapsed momentarily. 'Why do you look so happy?' he growled at fake Roger.

'Ha! Ha! Heh! Heh! Hi! Hi!' was all the astounded Farkheem heard in response.

'You are just about to suffer a terrible, torturous death and you are laughing?' the president snarled.

Fake Roger seemed to find this hilarious and burst into uproarious non-stop laughter. Everyone in the hall braced themselves for an explosion of rage by the insane dictator. Instead, Farkheem's face contorted into a comical grimace as he tried to stop from laughing himself. But fake Roger's hysterical cackling was just too infectious, and the president finally gave in and burst out laughing. Everyone in the hall visibly relaxed and soon the entire hall was filled with roaring laughter as people completely lost control of themselves. Even Dr Folterknecht laughed—a repetitive, weird, yelping hyena laugh, followed by a snort.

Fake Roger, still cackling hysterically, slowly moved backwards for a short distance then casually turned around and headed towards the entrance.

'The—Ha! Ha! Ha! Snort!—prisoner is esca—Ha! Ha! Ha! Snort!—Shoo . . . shoot—Ha! Ha! Ha! Snort!—him!' stammered Dr Folterknecht.

Too late! Fake Roger reached the entrance unhindered. Only the heavy CLONK of the huge steel bar used to lock the massive front doors from the outside finally stopped people laughing.

After about fifteen seconds of stunned silence, Ido Farkheem thundered at his guards, 'Catch him, you idiots!'

Dr Folterknecht zoomed out the small back door eager to apprehend fake Roger, followed by about a hundred guards in single file. When they all reached the front entrance, Folterknecht fell flat on his backside, having stepped on a white pebble which had, seconds earlier, been the fake Roger robot. Boots seemed to be a magnet for this pebble; it brought dozens of guards down before it became airborne and flew through a huge stained-glass window depicting an image of President Ido. The window shattered completely, and the pebble was gone.

'Sabotage!' screeched the mad doctor, beside himself with rage. 'Find him! Yah! Find him immediately! Yah!'

HACK
WHACK
KICK
KICK

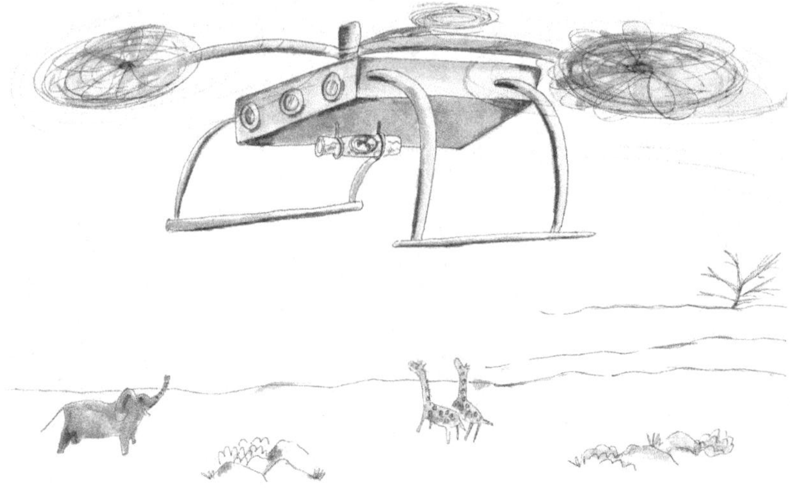

14

Inside the hall, the president was having a temper tantrum, throwing chairs around and shouting wildly, giving a convincing impersonation of a deranged mountain gorilla. 'That's it! Let's do it!' he bellowed. 'World domination! We make Roganda great again! To the broadcasting room!'

He rushed off with his personal aides, followed by Dr Folterknecht, to a specially prepared television studio. Make-up artists immediately started the challenging task of making Farkheem's ugly face presentable for television. The mad doctor, though, refused this treatment. Camera crews readied themselves while the crazy dictator was dressed up in a ridiculously extravagant golden coat and a pretentious hat made to resemble a glittering, bejewelled crown. Somehow, President Farkheem had deluded himself that the television audience would be impressed with such an absurd flamboyance.

One audience the brutal dictator wasn't trying to impress, and knew nothing about, was at a campsite in Kinkanza Nature Park. Andy, Johann and the real Roger Less sat in a darkened room watching with amazement the three-dimensional vision Michaela was providing of the unfolding drama at Ido Farkheem's palace.

It felt to them like they were actually there in the middle of the action.

Dr Folterknecht was the first one to sit in front of the cameras. He took his place on a small wooden chair beside the crazy dictator's golden throne.

Once the president sat down, the cameras started rolling. 'I have a dream!' Farkheem proclaimed with shameless imitation. 'A dream for a better world . . . under Roganda!' He paused to give added emphasis to his next statement. 'I know many of you watching will be smiling at such outrageous ambition. Who does he think he is? I can hear you saying. But to show you I know exactly who I am, and how serious I am, I will ask my good friend Dr Wueterich Folterknecht, the future leader of Teutonia, to explain the two choices you have.'

'Yah!' the mad doctor yelped at the camera with high-pitched excitement. 'The choices are simple! Yah! You either join our quest for world domination, or you perish! Yah! A no-brainer! Yah! Forget your armies, nuclear bombs and whatever else you might have! They will be useless! Yah! I have developed an invisible weapon of mass destruction that has the potential to kill every living thing on this planet! Yah! Except the Rogandan and Teutonian armies of course! Yah!' He paused to try and contain his excitement a little and bring the pitch of his voice down a few octaves. 'I shall demonstrate the truth of what I say by releasing a small dose of the deadly virus in Kinkanza's famous national nature park, eliminating every animal there, including any human ones who don't leave now! Yah! After this demonstration, world leaders will have one week to sign the agreement to join us in our quest and put a new world order in place! Yah! Yah!' After another short pause to calm himself, he said, 'And to the Government of Teutonia I have a special proclamation . . . I shall order the extermination of all stupid, useless pets . . . and forbid any further breeding of them! Yah! No more scratching cats! Yah! No more biting dogs! Yah! Not a single flea-bitten mutt or moggie to be seen! Yah! Teutonia will be a pet-free paradise! Yah!'

'He's gone completely nuts!' gasped Andy, watching at the campsite yet feeling he was right there in person.

'No, he's always been completely nuts,' Michaela corrected him. 'He's just taken it to new hysterical level that I'm sure your brain scientists don't even have a name for yet.'

Andy, Michaela and Roger watched the manic Dr Folterknecht turn to a big screen behind him. On it appeared a drone being fitted with a small device. The drone was then launched into the air above Kinkanza Nature Park and immediately began sending back pictures of various wild animals grazing contentedly. The doctor turned back to the camera and held up a small electronic device. 'This remote detonator will release the lethal virus into Kinkanza Nature Park. Yah! Every animal there will be killed within six hours! Yah!' Handing the remote to Ido Farkheem, he said, 'I give my dear friend President Farkheem the honour of releasing the first dose of mass destruction! Yah! Which will send a message to the whole world! Yah! A statement of proof that our capacity to destroy the world is undisputed! Yah!'

So saying, he handed the remote over to the absurd president of Roganda, who was trying to look regal and serene. However, the second he got the remote in his hand all pretense of regal serenity evaporated: he broke into a broad grin, like a little boy with a new toy. He beamed with evil anticipation and then burst into maniacal laughter. 'This one little button,' he sounded off, 'will change the world!' He doubled over with laughter: 'Huuuhhh! Ha! Ha! Ha! Bye-bye Kinkanza tourist industry! Huuuhhh! Ha! Ha! Ha! I am the undisputed greatest leader in the world. I am totally awesome!' He raised his hand and pressed the button, detonating a tiny explosion on the device attached to the drone.

'Success! Yah!' Dr Folterknecht squealed triumphantly.

The insane dictator and the mad doctor shook hands for the camera, and the broadcast ended. The excited president returned to his palace headquarters to prepare for the expected flood of calls from world leaders begging to join his quest. Folterknecht scurried back to the laboratories announcing that it would take at least six hours for the lethal virus to start taking effect.

15

At the campsite in Kinkanza Nature Park, Andy and the others were glued to their television screen with astonishment and disbelief. When the broadcast abruptly ceased, Roger leapt up and grabbed his special secret service cell phone.

'I must urgently advise the Britonnian government to ignore this threat!' he cried. 'They need to know the virus is harmless!'

'No!' Michaela said firmly. 'What's the point of telling them to ignore something they don't even know about?'

'What?' Roger exclaimed. 'But that telecast would have been seen worldwide!'

'It wasn't,' Michaela answered calmly. 'I put a shield around their transmission site; they can't transmit more than two kilometres in any direction. When Ido Farkheem reaches his palace in a couple of hours, no one there will have seen anything of what we just witnessed. Neither will anybody else anywhere in the world.'

'Brilliant!' Roger gasped.

'Thank you,' Michaela replied dryly, unaccustomed to any praise from the famous secret agent.

'So, it's all over?' Andy asked, hopeful.

'Unfortunately, not!' Michaela responded sternly. 'Once Farkheem realises that Folterknecht's formula doesn't work and his dream of world domination is shattered, he will revert to his original plan, which was to begin with conquering Kinkanza. I estimate that in three days, at the very latest, the troops at his secret military base will cross the border and move towards Calisburg.'

'That would be tens of thousands of well-armed soldiers to contend with!' a dismayed Roger exclaimed.

'That will be our task!' Roger heard Michaela say, not quite believing his ears. 'We have to visit their base today,' she added, 'render their missiles useless . . . and ground their air force. That's all!'

'And their army?' retorted Roger. Andy was thinking the same thing.

'Leave that to me,' Michaela said. 'That's the easy bit.'

'This, I have to see,' Roger muttered, shaking his head in disbelief.

'You will!' Michaela countered, stretching out her arms. 'Both of you, hold my hands!' ZAP! An instant later they found themselves on a mountain top overlooking Ido Farkheem's secret military base.

Inside the castle built into the side of the mountain, Dr Folterknecht was carefully analyzing a small sample of his deadly red liquid, with Idi Amonia looking over his shoulder. To avoid contaminating the area, the sample had to be handled only by robotic arms behind thickened glass. When the mad doctor finally managed to place his sample under a powerful microscope, he got the shock of his life. Instead of looking at a liquid teeming with deadly viruses, he could see absolutely nothing alive in his sample. Sweat began pouring from his forehead and dripping off his nose. He started to shake. 'Sabotage . . . sabotage, yah,' he whispered.

With a quick move of the robotic arm, the panic-stricken doctor swiped the sample off the microscope to ensure Dr Amonia couldn't examine it.

'What are you doing, Doctor?' Amonia cried, visibly upset.

'My apologies, Idi! Yah! But sometimes when I examine my creation microscopically it terrifies me so much that I break out in a sweat and lose control! Yah!'

Amonia didn't look convinced but gave his fellow doctor the benefit of the doubt.

'Idi,' Folterknecht said, desperately trying to maintain his composure, 'please prepare another sample and we will analyze it together. Yah!' He knew this would give him about an hour in which to escape; his friend President Farkheem had zero tolerance for failure, even by good friends.

Once Dr Amonia had gone Folterknecht rushed down to the control room, announcing that he needed all his men for a secret expedition ordered by the president himself. The general in charge didn't question him. He even provided them a vehicle.

'I will be back in three hours,' Dr Folterknecht squeaked. 'In time to watch the animals in the park dying! Yah!'

Minutes later, the Teutonia Secret Police chief and his goons were racing for their lives towards the Kinkanza border.

Meanwhile, the insane Rogandan dictator Farkheem was in his palace impatiently pacing the presidential suite, waiting for world leaders to call him in their desperation to join his quest for world domination. His angry face suddenly beamed with happiness when one of his aides informed him that President Numbskull was on the phone asking to speak with him.

'Ah! See now!' he gloated, 'The president of the New Colonies has come crawling and begging to me! Ha! Ha! Ha! Put him through . . . on speakerphone.'

'Hello, Ido my friend!' the voice of President Numbskull boomed though the speaker. 'Have I got a deal for you!'

'I'm listening,' Farkheem replied, slapping his thigh with excitement.

'I hear you had a situation, and your two warships were badly damaged,' Numbskull said.

President Farkheem's face turned from beaming to stunned to enraged in the space of two seconds. He glared at one of his aides, who instantly broke out in such a sweat it started pouring down his face.

'No, not at all,' Farkheem finally replied, trying to keep the shock and rage out of his voice. 'Minor damage! Very minor!'

'Anyway,' Numbskull continued, 'listen carefully! I'm prepared to sell you two near-new frigates! And because you are a friend of mine, I will throw in two helicopters for free! That's the deal of a lifetime, Ido Farkheem!'

Farkheem began to shake. 'Did you see my telecast?'

'What telecast?'

Farkheem flew into a wild rage, grabbing the speakerphone and slamming it against the wall, shattering it to pieces. Almost at the same instant, the door opened, and an aide ran in with a replacement phone. Phone smashing was a common occurrence with the crazy president. His phones survived just three calls each, on average, so his aides kept a supply of a hundred new phones in reserve.

The phone-throwing president was now throwing a massive temper tantrum, stomping about screaming and crying. The new phone didn't escape; it too was smashed against the wall. After repeating the performance with four further replacements, the loony dictator began to calm down.

'I gave orders to copy the telecast!' he shouted. 'Get me a copy now!'

When his aides told him that no telecast was received in their city, that there was nothing to copy, Farkheem lost it completely, almost fainting with fury and disbelief. 'Sabotage!' he wailed. 'Subversion! Rebellion! A revolt against me! Get me General Mambo on the phone!' A shiny new phone was already in place. The aides had secretly taken bets on how long it would last. They tried to contact General Mambo, but to no avail—all communication lines in and out of the presidential palace were dead. Michaela's magic shield was still working perfectly.

President Farkheem smelled betrayal and became fearful of a revolution and coup against him. He decided to drive to his secret military base, considering it safer than taking a helicopter, and ordered his closest aides to join him. He suspected General Mambo of treason and wanted to surprise him.

16

Roger was still a bit shaken; he couldn't quite come to terms with teleportation. Military matters always got him focused though, so when Michaela questioned him about the army base stretched out below them, he quickly recovered. He knew what kind of missiles they had and their range and effects, as he did with their jets and other armaments.

Michaela was especially curious about whether their missiles were radio-controlled or operated by satellite navigation systems.

'They're radio-controlled,' Roger told her.

'Excellent!' Michaela said.

'We still have to destroy the detonators in all the missiles . . . twenty-two of them.' Roger scowled. 'In order to do that we would have to take the top section of each missile apart to reach the wires, then put them back together again. That would take at least a day, with a high risk of being detected.'

'Not a problem!' said Michaela, laughing. 'You just have to show me the first one! Andy, you stay here.' She took Roger's hand, and ZAP! They were gone.

Andy barely had time to get bored because five minutes later they were back again.

'We would have taken a lot less time,' Michaela complained, 'if Roger hadn't freaked out so much!'

'Who wouldn't freak out?' Roger roared. 'Andy, I suddenly found myself shrunk to microscopic size, surrounded by zillions of bacteria and various other creepy crawly microscopic creatures that looked like monsters from a Martian horror movie! It was worse than being turned into a goat!' He turned to Andy for sympathy, but Andy was staying clear of their argument.

'Yes, harmless bacteria and organisms,' Michaela scolded.

'The wires in the missiles were like giant tree trunks!' Roger wailed. 'Then she enlarged me slightly, which was a bit better, except that it squashed my head between two giant tree-trunk wires, and while I was trying to extricate my head, she was asking me to tell her which wires to cut! Then she shrank me to microscopic size again and told me to wait . . . right on top of zillions of those horrible little microbes squirming and crawling under me . . . moving me along like I was standing on molten lava! Only a blind moron wouldn't freak out!'

'Stop whining, you big baby,' Michaela scolded. 'I didn't take long!'

'Two seconds was too long!' Roger cried, still reliving the horror.

'Back to work!' Michaela called out, ignoring Roger's histrionics. 'Now to the fighter jets, Roger! What would be the best way to render them useless?'

'Oh no! Good grief!' Roger cried. 'I'm not diving into any jet engines to bend the blades! I've had enough!' He jumped away from Michaela. 'Don't touch me!'

'No need!' laughed Michaela. 'Just tell me which parts to bend or destroy and where they're located in the engines.'

A mightily relieved Roger answered Michaela's questions in precise detail . . . then she was gone.

A minute later she was back. 'Oh,' she said, 'what about the artillery canons?'

'The firing mechanism,' Roger replied, safely positioning himself behind Andy. 'Cut any wires connected to it.'

'Done!' Michaela said as she reached around Andy and teasingly pretended to try and touch Roger. Then she was gone once again.

'She doesn't mess around, that one!' Roger said with begrudging admiration.

Michaela was back so fast she heard his remark and smiled to herself. 'Our work is done!' she cheerfully announced.

'What about this other tiny problem?' Roger smirked, still not prepared to let her off the hook. 'Just the small matter of thirty thousand heavily armed troops ready to cross the border!'

'Humans are no problem to me!' Michaela chirped. 'That's the easy part!'

Roger's smirk instantly faded. Andy just laughed.

'Let's go back,' Michaela said, holding out both hands.

'Oh no!' Roger whined, shaking his head. He hesitantly took hold of Michaela's outstretched hand. ZAP! The next moment they were back at the nature park campsite.

Michaela immediately dematerialised and slipped back into the pencil. Roger had to lie down, still quite shaken by his experience. Andy was tired too, but he first went to the restaurant kitchen and collected leftover food to feed the many animals, including wild dogs, big cats, zebras, antelopes and numerous birds that hung around his cabin—but only his cabin. Others, especially the rangers, noticed this phenomenon and observed, with astonishment, birds landing on Andy's shoulders and some of the wild animals taking food from his hand. They watched even the most venomous snakes, like black mambas and puff adders, seeming to befriend this unusual young man.

'Dolittle! Just Dolittle!' Professor Katz-Kopf proudly explained to anyone listening.

Early the next morning, the usual dawn chorus of bird and animal sounds was drowned out by a loud argument between the commander of the anti-poaching unit and seven men in black suits and red ties.

'You can't enter Kinkanza like this!' bellowed the commander. 'And especially in a Rogandan Army truck!'

'I'm the head of the Teutonia Secret Police, you underling!' A red-faced Dr Folterknecht was shouting, getting more heated and flushed by the second. 'Get out of my way or I will arrest you! Yah!'

'Sorry!' barked the commander. 'I have to impound your truck and hand you over to the Kinkanza authorities. You and your men are under arrest!'

At that moment, Roger happened to walk by on his way to the breakfast buffet. Spotting the mad doctor, he grinned and called out, 'Folterknecht! You won't like it here. . . . They don't serve sauerkraut for breakfast!'

'Roger Less!' screeched Folterknecht and, turning to his men, ordered them to arrest Roger. 'Cuff him and put him in chains! Yah! And this man too! Yah!' He pointed at the commander.

The doctor's six goons drew their pistols and charged—two of them at the commander and four at Roger. The secret agent raised his hands as if surrendering, but when the first two men were within reach, Roger skillfully disarmed them and pushed them into the other two men. All four attackers collapsed to the ground, holding their heads in pain after bumping into each other in the scuffle.

The other two goons managed to handcuff the commander before turning their guns on Roger, but by this time Andy had arrived on the scene. With his super speed, he disarmed both men, uncuffed the commander, and used the cuffs on Folterknecht. The commander's anti-poaching men then quickly pushed the mad doctor and his henchmen into a large cage reserved for apprehended poachers.

'Treason! Yah!' screeched Folterknecht, wildly rattling the cage.

17

At the same time, across the border in Roganda, President Ido Farkheem was fully intending to put his army chief, General Mambo, in a cage as well. But just as he reached the outskirts of his military base, his phone started ringing. It was General Mambo, desperately trying to reach his president. 'There has been a total breakdown of our communications system,' the general explained.

Mambo managed to convince the insane dictator there was no coup—and the beads of sweat on the general's forehead slowly evaporated.

Stunned but relieved, Farkheem rushed to his laboratory complex where he was soon joined by General Mambo. As the two men entered the control room, a frenzied Dr Idi Amonia ran after them yelling, 'Fraud! Fraud!'

'This control room is in lockdown!' Farkheem shouted, waving his arms around in a fury as the door shut behind him. Then to General Mambo he barked, 'Update! Update! Now!'

The general fired up the big video screen and tried his best to explain what had happened . . . or more correctly, hadn't happened. He pointed to the drone pictures of the vast herds of animals in Kinkanza Nature Park still very much alive and grazing contentedly.

'That cannot be!' the crazy dictator roared, becoming more and more infuriated. 'Get me Folterknecht now!'

Two of Farkheem's aides raced out to find the mad doctor. As they opened the door, an over-excited Dr Amonia charged in, holding aloft Folterknecht's small vial of red liquid. In the doctor's triumphant exuberance to reveal the liquid was useless, he stumbled over a chair, fell heavily and dropped the vial. It shattered into a thousand tiny pieces, spreading the red liquid all over the floor.

'You murderous fool!' gurgled President Farkheem as he ran out and slammed the door, locking it from the outside in the hopes of containing the lethal virus to the control room. It seemed of no concern to him that he was the only one who got out. Suddenly there was utter panic in the room as everyone thought they were trapped and doomed to an agonising death by a chemical weapon.

General Mambo's eyes were like saucers as he peered out at Farkheem through a small window. His eyes then rolled back in his head, and he passed out from sheer terror.

'Wow! That stuff works fast!' the lunatic dictator gasped. 'Excellent! Very impressive!'

Finally recovering from his tumble, Idi Amonia got to his feet and yelled at the top of his voice, 'Stop! Stop panicking! The red liquid is less dangerous than apple juice!'

'Never thought apple juice was so dangerous,' President Farkheem mumbled, still not quite understanding the situation.

'Dr Folterknecht is a fraud!' hollered Dr Amonia. 'The liquid is a dud! It wouldn't kill a sick mosquito!'

The dictator, now understanding his plan was foiled, opened the door so Dr Amonia could hear his full rant. He threw the temper tantrum of the year. It was possible the whole valley heard his screams, but all his rage was focused on one man, Dr Folterknecht.

When Farkheem's aides returned to inform their leader that the mad doctor had escaped from Roganda, the president suffered a nervous breakdown. It took him several hours to recover, after which he immediately returned to his military base. He stormed into his situation room, his face flickering with anger and announced, 'Tomorrow evening I will have a celebratory dinner in Calisburg, Kinkanza, because tomorrow morning we invade the country! Our army can be there in eight hours! We will arrive like a lightning strike! They won't know what hit them! Uh! Ha! Ha! Ha!'

Everyone in the room laughed along with him and clapped and cheered for good measure.

General Mambo, now recovered, called his officers for a briefing and soon the whole valley was seething with activity, preparing for the invasion.

Andy was busy with his own activities. He was out on an expedition with his group, tracking and observing lion families. He had just settled in to study one large pride when he heard the magic pencil talking to him telepathically.

'President Farkheem will make his move tomorrow,' it said. 'Here is our plan!'

Andy listened carefully, his face frequently breaking into a big smile. Once the pencil had finished outlining the plan, an excited Andy cried out, 'I'm ready!'

'Ready for what?' enquired his professor, who was sitting next to him. He scowled with understandable concern. 'Dolittle! We don't want any trouble!'

'No worries, Professor!' Andy said. He flashed the professor a smile and went back to observing the lions through his binoculars, secretly looking forward to the next day.

Dawn seemed to take forever but finally soft pink light started to colour the sky, and Andy leapt out of bed, rearing to go. Roger wasn't far behind him and then the beautiful Michaela materialised from the pencil. She looked happy and relaxed. 'Let's have some fun!' she chirped. Positioning herself between Roger and Andy, she grabbed their hands and swung them up over her head. ZAP! They were instantly standing on a small hill overlooking the Kinkanza border.

'I still can't get used to this teleportation!' Roger complained. But he was quickly distracted by the approaching Rogandan army. 'What a sight!' he exclaimed, impressed with the thousands of military vehicles, including transporters, Jeeps and other armoured motorised ordnance, forming an endless line of destructive war machines all rolling towards the Kinkanza border.

'Shall we take out the first couple of vehicles?' Andy enquired, readying himself.

'No, not necessary,' Michaela replied, vanishing into thin air as she said it.

'Where did she go now?' Roger mumbled.

'There!' Andy cried out, pointing frantically with one hand and grasping his binoculars with the other.

All Roger could make out was a tall man in a Rogandan general's uniform standing at the border waving to the armoured convoy. 'That's President Farkheem!' Roger shouted all excited. 'Let's get him!'

'No, Roger!' Andy cried. 'That figure just materialised there. It's the spirit of my magic pencil—Michaela in the guise of Ido Farkheem. She can transform into anything . . . or anyone.'

When the leaders of the advancing army saw what they assumed was their president in his glittering army uniform, they halted the convoy. Soldiers began rushing from their vehicles and bowing before their leader.

Andy and Roger then heard the 'president's' voice in their heads as clearly as the soldiers crowded around him. 'This is your president speaking to all of you as a fellow soldier,' the magic pencil in the form of Ido Farkheem announced. 'My friends! My comrades! Our secret service has detected a deadly virus present in Kinkanza, and I cannot risk exposing you all to it! And so, breaking with all military rules, I am making an emergency presidential decree to send you all home immediately! Turn your convoy around now and go back. You will be home by dinnertime! Tomorrow will be a presidential holiday, fully paid!'

Wild cheering and applause filled the air as masses of army vehicles began turning around and heading back to where they came from. Then came the last, curious proclamation from the president that each and every soldier could hear clearly in his head, 'I want you to forget my face—forget that I exist at all. I want you to elect a new leader of Roganda in a democratic vote! Out with dictatorship! In with the Democratic Republic of Roganda! Freedom and respect for all Rogandans!

The deafening cheer of thousands of soldiers rang out from the departing convoy.

'Wow!' gasped Roger. 'She turned a whole army around without a single shot being fired!'

'And turned a dictatorship into a democracy at the same time!' Andy cried, punching the air with his fists.

18

Meanwhile, close to the Kinkanza border, at a safe distance behind the rest of his army, the real President Ido Farkheem was issuing final orders to his Rocket Missile Detachment. His intention was to shock and awe. He would stun the Kinkanza population into surrender.

'Fire!' he screeched.

Rocket after rocket exploded from the mobile launchers and streaked towards the Kinkanza capital of Calisburg. With each fearsome firing of a rocket the insane dictator clapped and giggled like a child watching clowns at a circus. 'Uh! Uh! Ha! Ha! Ha!' he shrieked. 'Calisburg will be burning!'

Once the barrage of twenty-two missiles was over, Farkheem roared triumphantly. 'Let's move out! Tonight, I want dinner in the Calisburg Palace! Ha! Ha! Ha!'

From their vantage point high on the hill, Andy, Roger and Michaela watched the missiles drop out of the sky, their radio guidance systems dysfunctional, thanks to Michaela. The rockets fell harmlessly into the sandy desert soil of the isolated borderlands without exploding, their detonators also disabled.

'Our work here is done!' Michaela declared cheerily as they all high-fived one another. Then, ZAP! They were back at the nature park camp.

Lounging back with supreme confidence and satisfaction in his big red open limousine, President Ido Farkheem headed off in the direction of Calisburg. With great satisfaction, he was picturing his all-conquering army somewhere in the distance ahead of him marching into the Kinkanza capital. But just as the limousine crossed into the isolated borderlands separating Roganda and Kinkanza, an astounding sight brought Farkheem's happy little convoy to an abrupt halt. There, all around him, a dumbfounded dictator saw his twenty-two rocket missiles stuck head-first in the sand, seemingly perfectly intact.

'Aaarrrrgh!' he thundered. 'More sabotage and betrayal!' He leapt from his car in a rage to inspect the missiles more closely. Shaking both fists in the air, he howled, 'I bought these from the Numbskull Corporation! Numbskull! Numbskull! You are a liar and a cheat!' Quickly returned to his car, he continued his journey deeper into Kinkanza, confident that even without the rockets creating shock and awe his army would have no trouble conquering Calisburg; he would still get to have dinner at the palace.

Andy, Roger and Michaela were enjoying afternoon tea after listening to a lecture from Professor Katz-Kopf. The tea put Roger to sleep, so he missed the first sighting of President Farkheem's bright-red stretch limo and accompanying military vehicles when the little convoy appeared on the horizon.

'Oh! Yes! Here we go!' Andy grinned. 'Time for some action!' He stabbed his finger pointedly at Michaela. 'And don't you do all of it alone again!'

'You'll get your chance, Andy,' Michaela responded firmly. 'Stay calm and listen to what I tell you.'

As it happened, the camp was quite empty of people. Following his lecture, Professor Katz-Kopf went out with his students and the anti-poaching unit to investigate a new site where fossilised bones had been discovered; other tourists were away on safari. It was only Andy and Roger who had stayed behind to get some much-needed rest.

Michaela poked Roger, asleep in his chair. 'Roger, President Farkheem's approaching. Stay out of sight. He will recognise you instantly!'

Moments later the dictator came to a halt right in the centre of the camp. 'Why hasn't this place been erased . . . burnt to the ground?' he shouted as he emerged from the red limo.

'Because we have a gift for you,' Michaela piped up, smiling radiantly at Farkheem.

'What? Oh . . . oh!' he stammered, seeing Michaela for the first time. 'You are beautiful! I will not only spare your life young lady, but I will also invite you to be my thirty-third wife! You will remember this as the best day of your life, my love!'

Michaela gave the lunatic a coy smile, as if she were complimented by this crass proposal, and then responded softly, 'First to business! We will hand Dr Wueterich Folterknecht over to you as long as you promise to leave this camp alone and not hurt a living soul . . . or animal.'

'Folterknecht!' the dictator screamed, pulling his pistol from its holster and waving it around. 'That treacherous rotten little swine! I will kill him! Burn him! Shoot him! Hang him! I will ...' He began stomping around like an infuriated toddler who couldn't get its own way. Fortunately, at this point, he was so incensed with rage and his voice became such a strident shriek that the obscenities flowing from his mouth were virtually unintelligible.

This demented performance was too much for Roger, who forgot Michaela's orders and showed himself. 'I say!' he exclaimed. 'What a disgusting perform—'

PANG! A bullet from Farkheem's gun took Roger in his chest. The secret agent hit the ground like a bag of wheat dropped from a height. He didn't move.

'The laughing man!' the loony dictator shouted. 'Won't laugh anymore! Uh! Uh! Ha! Ha! Ha! So funny!'

Blind with rage, Andy was just about to attack Farkheem when he heard Michaela's voice in his head. 'Stop, Andy! I gave Roger nine lives . . . remember? He still has eight left!'

Andy instantly calmed down and started to lead the murderous madman to the building where the possibly even madder Dr Folterknecht and his six henchmen were being held as prisoners.

They had only gone a few paces when Andy was dismayed to hear the words 'I say!' He turned to see Roger getting to his feet.

PANG! Farkheem fired another bullet into Roger's chest. The secret agent collapsed in a heap once again. The dictator just shook his head in amazement, then laughed again.

'Seven left,' Michaela's voice declared dryly in Andy's head. 'We have to keep this sparrow-brained Britonnian, this confused noodlehead, down once he's been shot! He's wasting his lives!'

When they reached their destination, the crazy Farkheem stopped and waved four of his soldiers into the building, their guns drawn. A minute later they gave the 'all clear' and the president hurried in after them, followed by Andy and Michaela. Roger had decided he didn't want to be shot dead a third time, so he stayed where he was, sprawled in the dust outside.

19

Once inside the building, President Farkheem rushed to the far corner where Andy had told him Dr Folterknecht was being held.

'Uh! Huh! Ha! Ha! Ha!' Farkheem roared when he saw the doctor, the two totally insane megalomaniacs having come face-to-face. 'You shall die a thousand deaths! No, two thousand! I will personally torture you. I will . . .' Again, fortunately, the dictator's subsequent hysterical, foul-mouthed abuse was unintelligible.

'I have been sabotaged!' Folterknecht squealed desperately. 'It was the aliens! Yah!'

'Uh! Ha! Ha! Ha!' barked Farkheem triumphantly. 'There is no such thing as aliens!'

At that point, Andy and Michaela caught up with Farkheem, who had bolted ahead of them to confront Folterknecht. Because of the mad doctor's continuous squealing of his innocence, he lost his voice with his last cry of the word 'alien'. All he could do was point wildly at Michaela.

'Stop pointing at my thirty-third wife-to-be . . . you obnoxious hyena!' Farkheem growled, grabbing Michaela's hand.

Big mistake! Suddenly the loony dictator was in the cage with the mad doctor. Farkheem was so busy stomping up and down and shouting abuse at Folterknecht that it took a while for him to realise his predicament.

Michaela then brought her spirit powers to bear on the behaviour of Farkheem's four soldiers standing with their guns drawn outside the cage. Acting like zombies, they dropped their weapons and started to walk out.

'Stop! Stop! Farkheem screamed after them, wildly stabbing his finger at everyone. 'Shoot them all! And let me out! Now! Instantly!'

His soldiers seemed not to hear him and kept walking away in a trance-like state, courtesy of Michaela.

'Hee! Hee! Hee! Hee!' yelped Folterknecht doing a good impersonation of the obnoxious hyena Farkheem earlier accused him of being. 'See! I told you! She is an alien! Yah!'

While Folterknecht continued his hyena giggling, and an enraged Farkheem kept rattling the cage, Michaela and Andy wandered outside to find Roger up on his feet and chatting to the other soldiers, who had all dropped their weapons. They all started jostling one another to shake Michaela's hand before climbing into their vehicles and heading back to Roganda.

'These soldiers,' Michaela explained to Andy and Roger, 'and the thirty thousand I sent back earlier, have forgotten President Ido Farkheem's face . . . and that he ever existed. And so will everyone else they come in contact with. Within a few weeks, every person in Roganda will have no memory whatsoever of their murderous, insane dictator.'

'Rather brilliant!' admitted Roger.

'But your behaviour was not!' Michaela scolded, rolling her eyes at the secret agent.

Roger was oblivious to the fact that he had been shot dead twice. When Andy explained it to him, the famous secret agent nearly died a third time, on the spot . . . from shock.

'You're lucky Michaela gave you nine lives a year ago because she was worried about your reckless disregard for the one you were born with,' Andy chided him.

Roger looked suitably chastened and had nothing to say.

'Now!' Michaela declared. 'We must get rid of our prisoners while everyone is still absent from camp. They are of no more use to us.' She handed a ring of keys to the camp's pet monkey and, in her own mysterious way, gave it instructions. The creature bounded into the building where Folterknecht and Farkheem were trapped in the cage. The two prisoners' voices were clearly audible outside as they tried to coax the monkey close to the cage.

'Good monkey!' said Farkheem. 'No! Bad monkey!'

'Come here and I will shower you with bananas!' added Folterknecht.

'Come here or I will shoot you!' threatened Farkheem.

Eventually, the monkey went up to the cage out of sheer curiosity. Farkheem grabbed the keys from the monkey's paw. 'Ha! Ha! Ha! Stupid monkey!' he screeched.

Half a minute later, Andy, Michaela and Roger watched as the lunatic dictator, the mad doctor and his six henchmen rushed from the building, the president with his pistol drawn desperately looking around for his soldiers. The only thing left that he recognised was his big red stretch limo, still parked in the middle of the camp. There was room enough for the eight of them, so they all started to clamber into the open-topped car.

Just as Farkheem was about to get in, Roger waved and called out, 'Bye! Bye!'

PANG! PANG! PANG! Click! Click! Click! Roger went down like a shot baboon, yet again.

But the three gun clicks hadn't escaped Folterknecht's attention. 'Hee! Hee! Hee! Farkheem's out of ammunition! Yah! Seize him! Take his gun away! Yah!' he screeched at his men as he jumped into the driver's seat. His six goons quickly disarmed Farkheem and knocked him to the ground while their boss gunned the engine of the big limo. The instant his men were all back on board, the mad doctor threw the limo into gear, planted his foot and roared off towards Calisburg without the president.

Farkheem, still fully expecting to catch up with his conquering army, shouted after the departing limo, shaking his fists, 'I will find you! Consider yourselves eradicated! Uh! Ha! Ha! Ha!'

'Nasty man!' Roger remarked as he got to his feet once again.

'Really? You think so?' Michaela said sarcastically, rolling her eyes.

Farkheem nearly fainted with anger and disbelief seeing Roger obviously uninjured. Fortunately, the dictator's gun was out of bullets, so Roger didn't waste another life. But with Michaela and Andy's attention momentarily on Roger, Farkheem stole an anti-poaching-squad vehicle and snuck his way out of camp, heading the same way his stolen limousine had gone.

20

The camp began to fill up with people again as everyone returned from their expeditions and safaris. Professor Katz-Kopf, his students and the anti-poaching unit all returned highly excited by their big discovery of fossilized bone.

The following day passed quickly—rather too quickly for Andy who very much loved observing nature. He was sorry the expedition was ending already. Roger left to meet up with Johann in Calisburg before heading back to Britonnia. And when Andy finally met up with his father the day after that, they took a short cruise south to a famous beach resort where Anna joined them for the last seven days of their holiday.

Life was no holiday for President Ido Farkheem, however. It was more like a nightmare. When he eventually reached the outskirts of Calisburg, exhausted and angry and saw no sign of an advancing army, he added total confusion to his agitated state of mind. Then he convinced himself that, finding no resistance, his army would have taken over the governing palace as he had ordered them to do. He skidded his stolen patrol vehicle to a halt in the street a short distance from the palace, attracting the attention of a squad of Teutonian police who were about to leave for the airport.

'I shall invite you to dinner with me in the palace!' he shouted at them as they approached, 'before I have you all shot!'

This did not go down so well with the police, who promptly kicked the unknown man out of the vehicle, which they then confiscated and took to the airport with them. Now on foot, Farkheem used his special phone and called a direct line to President Numbskull of the New Colonies to inform him of his conquest of Kinkanza.

'Hello . . . *Boni*? It's Ido,' he announced.

'Who? Fido? Anyone with a dog's name is a loser . . . or a lunatic . . . probably barking mad! Ha! Ha! Ha!' Numbskull didn't realise how precisely accurate his corny joke was. 'How did you get this number? Bad! Very bad!' CLICK!

'Fido? Fido?' Farkheem screeched. 'Moron! Bonehead! No wonder your name is Numbskull!' At this point the president started to lose it a bit and threw his phone into the oncoming traffic, smashing the windshield of a police patrol car.

That was a mistake. Within minutes, Farkheem was surrounded by police officers.

'Kneel before your president!' Farkheem demanded.

None of the officers seemed willing to oblige. Instead, two of them handcuffed him and put him in the back of a patrol car. All the way to their destination, Farkheem loudly proclaimed that he had conquered Kinkanza and was now their president and that they would all be shot. When the vehicle stopped, six men in white coats were there to greet Farkheem.

'Hello, Mr President!' one of the men said, bowing deeply. 'Welcome to your new palace!'

This instantly cheered up Farkheem.

'Your Highness,' another white-coated man said, 'Dr Friederich Himmelfart is looking forward to examin—sorry, welcoming you!'

When a now much calmer and happier Farkheem entered the building, he was nonetheless duly tasered and then injected with a sedative. It would take several years of psychological testing before the former tyrannical dictator of Roganda would receive Dr Himmelfart's final diagnosis: 'Not insane, just stupid.'

A short time after Farkheem was taken into custody, Dr Folterknecht, who was certainly insane and probably stupid as well, snuck back into Teutonia. He immediately started to work on reproducing his evil chemical and viral concoctions, which he had lost through the 'alien' Michaela's sabotage. With that particular alien in his mind, the doctor also intensified his research efforts into finding ways of capturing and harnessing her incredible, unearthly powers. He decided his test target would be the unsuspecting town of Stone.

21

While the mad Dr Folterknecht was trying to unlock the mysteries of alien powers, the police in Snobtown were baffled by a much more mundane mystery. In just one week they had reports of two hundred wallets and thirty-five handbags stolen, with no sign of the crafty thief. The pilfering mystery would have been solved in an instant had they known about the secret treasure room Countess Kunnikunde had had built beneath her house. It was a large space, containing huge pots of gold coins, shelving stacked with handbags and wallets—too many to count—and golden bathtubs overflowing with money, as well as see-through pillow slips filled with gold nuggets and a sofa totally covered with thousand-dollar bills.

The treasure room was Kunnikunde's favourite retreat. Like a human Scrooge McDuck, she would dance around the room and hug and kiss her money. She even talked to it as if it were alive, declaring her deep love to the lifeless coins and paper bills. Kunnikunde was right in the middle of smooching and cooing to her money, when Lucifer suddenly appeared, startling her so much that she momentarily took her eyes off her money. Recovering quickly, she grabbed the devil's hand and led him to the only one of the many golden bathtubs that wasn't overflowing with money.

'The issue I have, Lucifer, is that I need money!' the countess wailed, pointing at the bathtub. 'This one is only half full!'

Shaking his head, the devil obliged. With his arm outstretched, one-thousand-dollar bills streamed out of his open hand, filling the tub in seconds.

'A little bit more, so that it overflows!' Kunnikunde demanded.

After a short burst of thousand-dollar bills into the tub, Lucifer sat down on the sofa.

'Get off my sofa!' Kunnikunde shrieked. 'Don't sit on my money! Get up! Get up! That's my money! Mine! Mine!'

The devil rolled his eyes and stood up and, with a flick of his hand, conjured a comfortable chair out of thin air. Sitting down, he rebuked the greedy countess. 'Kunnikunde, I wish you would put your stealing habit on hold for a while! Eighty percent of the population of Snobtown worships me! They help me create misery for all the obnoxious do-gooders and believers out there! They help me pollute the environment! They have no empathy for others and think only of themselves! These people are the essence of my existence! When you're stealing their wallets and handbags, it's distracting them from doing my dirty work for me!'

'I'm stealing from the rich to give to the poor!' Kunnikunde declared.

'What poor?' the devil asked.

'Me! Yes . . . I'm poor!' Kunnikunde wailed, putting her head in her hands. 'I'm broke! You have no idea!'

It was hard to tell whether the devil was more astounded or frustrated. 'Aaarrrrgh!' he screeched. 'You're appalling! However, I have to admit that it is your truly obscene obsession with money and addiction to stealing other people's money that attracts me so much to you! You may be the greediest and most selfish woman who ever lived! Congratulations!'

Kunnikunde wasn't sure if that was a compliment or not. She made no comment as she readjusted the thousand-dollar bills on the sofa the devil had disturbed when he sat on them.

Shaking his head again, Lucifer continued. 'The little black cloud above your head told me that—'

'That's it! You're spying on me with that accursed cloud! You have robbed me of my privacy!' She looked up at the little black blob above her head. 'I want this useless cloud gone! It's cramping my style! Get rid of it—now!'

'That could be unwise,' the devil responded calmly. 'That cloud contains a very powerful spirit. It is not only deadly, but it can detect traps as well as most other spiritual abnormalities—such as clones and other tricks of junior spirits.'

'See!' Kunnikunde yelled. 'That is exactly your problem, Lucifer! You complicate everything and fail! I have set a trap! And my laser power can reduce a thousand families to ashes! I don't need any help from that vile little spying monster!' She suddenly calmed down and put on the charm. 'Please, Lucifer, I beg you, take it away. Please!'

'OK,' the devil reluctantly agreed. 'As long as you understand that should you fail, it was your decision and responsibility.'

'Of course!' Kunnikunde chirped. 'I'm used to doing everything myself anyway!' She watched happily as the little black cloud above her head disappeared into the devil's hand. Her good mood was short-lived, however, when Lucifer threatened that if she didn't stop stealing from people in Snobtown he would start setting her money alight, bill by bill, and turning her gold coins to lead, one by one.

That worked. Realising he meant what he said, Kunnikunde decided to completely focus on her evil plan to eliminate her brother-in-law Johann and his family.

22

Mr Broombridge was on a spying mission for his beloved Countess. Impeccably dressed in what he considered perfectly suitable attire—a khaki safari suit and matching pith helmet—he set up camp at the edge of the forest right across from Johann's house. A warm, roomy tent with an air mattress, comfortable camping chairs and numerous cameras on tripods aimed at the house completed the scene. With binoculars hanging around his neck, Mr Broombridge busily worked at setting up a small drone fitted with a camera; he was confident this was the perfect final touch to his devious and despicable spying mission. The only slight flaw in this perfect set-up was that Mr Broombridge had never operated a drone.

Once he had the drone prepared to his satisfaction, he looked through his binoculars to do a quick check of Johann's house. He could see Andy's two dogs resting on the front porch; otherwise, there was no sign of life.

In Mr Broombridge's first clumsy attempt to fly the drone, he had trouble controlling the elevation. The drone was flying erratically across the house's expansive lawn only a few feet off the ground. This was irresistible prey for Sassy and Sally. Both dogs leapt off the porch and shot after the strange metal bird. With bits of earth and grass flying behind them, they raced madly across the lawn with frenzied acceleration.

Mr Broombridge was frantically trying to get the drone higher off the ground. Too late! Sassy, the white bull terrier, ripped the drone out of the air.

'Oh no!' gasped Mr Broombridge. 'That was a mistake!'

Sally, meanwhile, was more interested in greeting people than chasing strange low-flying birds. The brindle Staffordshire terrier headed full speed towards its frantic pilot. Sally, like other dogs of her breed, fancied herself as a lightweight, fleet-footed lapdog rather than a barrelling muscular bag of cement. Often incapable of stopping when she intended to, Sally collided with the impeccably dressed camper at full force. Mr Broombridge was lifted bodily from his chair. He crashed heavily on his back on the forest floor with Sally on top of him exuberantly licking his face.

'Bad dog! Bad dog! Get off me!' bellowed Mr Broombridge. No longer a picture of sartorial splendour, his once-immaculate shirt was covered in dirty paw marks and torn in several places. Happy with her friendly greeting, Sally finally got off Mr Broombridge and ran back to join Sassy, but not before biting Broombridge's pith helmet in two, thinking it was some kind of toy. Sassy by now had transformed the small drone into a clump of twisted metal with absolutely zero aerodynamics. Delighted with their work, the dogs toddled back to the porch to rest after such an energetic burst of activity.

Poor Mr Broombridge, who hated animals, especially the small, boisterous barking variety, abandoned his campsite and raced straight to the hospital emergency ward. He burst into reception yelling at the top of his voice, 'I have rabies! I was licked by a dog . . . on the face!'

After getting a dressing-down by the head nurse for unnecessarily causing a disturbance and wasting their time, she added, 'The dog's tongue would have been cleaner than your own!'

Horrified at the thought, Mr Broombridge staggered out of the hospital and rushed immediately to the Big City clothing store. Under normal circumstances, he would have spent many hours in front of the mirrors trying on countless different shirts and suits. That was his favourite pastime; but today was different. Anxious not to let Countess Kunnikunde down, he was focused only on getting a new suit and getting out of the store as fast as possible and back to his post. Racing through the store, he quickly found a replacement suit and hurried to the change rooms.

Mr. Broombridge's day was going from bad to worse. In his rush, he barged into a change room that was already occupied and bumped into the abundant behind of a large, semi-dressed lady whose head then hit the cubicle wall.

'You!' the lady shrieked when she turned and recognised her assailant. The ear-splitting cry of 'PERVERT!' echoed throughout the store, followed by sounds like gun shots. The formidable Lady Heger-Steel, the fearsome slapping machine, started slapping poor Mr Broombridge with her usual brutal ferocity—first with several strikes to his face followed by a flurry of blows to his backside. He ultimately managed to escape with a repeat of the word 'PERVERT!' ringing in his ears. Finally making it back to his forest hideout, he was in too much pain to sit in a chair or lie down on his air mattress.

23

Andy had a wonderful time with his parents at the beach resort. His father was in such a holiday mood that he decided he and Anna should go home by ship instead of flying so his wife could experience the pleasures of an ocean cruise for the first time. Andy was to fly home with his fellow students and Professor Katz-Kopf and would arrive three weeks before his parents returned. Andy suspected that his father's decision to prolong his holiday wasn't only so Anna could enjoy a cruise but also because the spirit of the magic pencil was back, in the form of Michaela. Johann wanted to keep his distance from her. Her presence made him extremely nervous and agitated.

Andy hated to think what his father's reaction would be if he knew about the incredible powers the pencil spirit had passed on to Andy. Fortunately, neither parent had any idea. And even though the guests at the resort knew nothing about that either, they were all impressed with how animals of all kinds responded to Andy.

There was one particular incident the guests would never forget. When two vicious guard dogs escaped from their enclosure and raced down to the beach with the intention of attacking anything that moved, Andy appeared out of nowhere, grabbed the snarling dogs and whispered in their ears. They immediately turned into gentle, friendly pooches. The bystanders applauded Andy with gratitude and amazement. Some guests also noticed that whenever Andy appeared on the balcony of his suite, the railing was suddenly lined with wild birds of all kinds.

When Andy finally waved his parents off on the cruise ship, Michaela appeared on the wharf beside him.

'Time to talk,' she said. 'There is a problem brewing. But I have a plan!'

'I'd be shocked if you didn't!' Andy chirped, delighted to see her.

At a café nearby, they talked for an hour. As Michaela revealed her plan, Andy laughed out loud several times. They then teleported themselves back to the special big barn that Michaela had constructed many years earlier. It included a large, comfortable apartment, in which they stayed overnight, keeping out of sight because it would be seen as impossible for Andy to be back home until the following day when his flight was due.

24

Mr Broombridge's swollen red face lit up with delight when he peered through his binoculars and saw Andy on the front porch of the house with the two crazy dogs. Almost rolling off his air mattress with excitement, he stumbled to his feet while frantically fumbling around for his phone. Dialling the number, Broombridge slumped onto a chair, momentarily forgetting his battered and bruised backside from his maltreatment at the hands of Lady Heger-Steel. An instant later he leapt up with a painful scream.

Holding the binoculars to his eyes with one hand and the phone with the other, he finally got through to Countess Kunnikunde, who appeared beside him a moment later. She yanked the binoculars from Broombridge's hands, nearly ripping his head off in the process with the strap that was around his neck. Freeing himself of the strap, he handed the binoculars to Kunnikunde, who immediately focused them on the house.

Andy's dogs Sassy and Sally were squealing with delight, running and jumping around in delirious celebration at the return of their beloved master.

Countess Kunnikunde observed this scene with mounting disgust. 'Where is Johann? Where is his creepy wife?' she wailed.

'They must be inside,' Mr Broombridge suggested.

Just then, Hermann and Fritz came out of the house to greet Andy. Kunnikunde was instantly suspicious. 'Go over there now!' she hissed at Mr Broombridge. 'Find out where Johann and his creepy wife are . . . and exactly when they will be home! Go! Go! Go!'

An intimidated Mr Broombridge hesitantly made his way over to the house. By the time he got there, everyone had gone inside, and he had to knock on the door. Sassy and Sally performed their duty of announcing the arrival of a visitor with such great energy and exuberance that Mr Broombridge shivered and had to force himself not to turn and run. He wasn't sure which was worse—the crazy, vicious dogs with their manic barking and growling or an enraged Kunnikunde. He decided it would be easier to face the dogs.

'I'll be right there!' he heard Andy yell out. Seconds later Andy appeared at the front door, keeping the dogs behind him.

'Greetings, Andy!' Mr Broombridge cried, affecting a cheery smile. 'My countess has a present for your family . . . a present of peace and love! She wants to make an appointment with all three of you as soon as possible.'

'Mum and Dad will be back in four days,' Andy announced with a friendly smile. 'I'm sure they would welcome my dear Aunt Kunnikunde for a cup of tea the afternoon they get back.' He knew full well they wouldn't be home for more than two weeks, but he was giving Mr Broombridge false information on Michaela's instructions.

'Wonderful! Thank you! Thank you!' Mr Broombridge gushed. 'And will you be here too, Andy?'

'Oh, yes!' Andy chirped. 'I wouldn't miss it for anything!'

'Excellent! Excellent!' Broombridge exclaimed excitedly then immediately rushed from the house back to the waiting Countess Kunnikunde. He took a circuitous route around the forest border to his secret spying hideout.

'Countess!' he yelled out as he approached the campsite. 'I have excellent news!'

Kunnikunde listened carefully but didn't seem to think it was particularly good news at all. 'I wouldn't have come and wasted a teleportation if I'd known only the boy was home . . . you incompetent fool!' she scolded.

'But Countess!' Mr Broombridge pleaded, desperately defending his actions. 'What about their last will and testament? That needs to be prepared in advance and will take several days!'

'OK,' Kunnikunde said, instantly mollified. 'Yes, good work, Broombridge. Now, book me a room in the Big City hotel. Tomorrow we shall see our lawyers!'

They left the secret hideout and took Mr Broombridge's car to the city. Kunnikunde drove. She had long ago refused to be driven anywhere by Broombridge after several terrifying near-death experiences as his passenger. On one occasion they had even ended up high in the branches of a large tree, still in his car.

Andy, meanwhile, had unpacked his bag and started looking for Michaela, who suddenly reappeared in the living room. 'Where were you?' he asked.

'Just saying hello to your aunt. I gave her a special flea bite designed to make her lose some control of her fire power. Let's hope it works!'

They moved to the dining room, where Fritz and Hermann had prepared a fine meal.

'Andy, did you have any interesting adventures on your trip?' Hermann asked.

Andy glanced at Michaela then took a big breath. 'Where should I start?'

It ended up being a long night.

Forgetting Satan's threat of removing her powers, Kunnikunde was distracted for a long time, too. On the way to the hotel, she stopped off at the shopping centre and spent several hours 'wallet shopping'. It was quite late when she decided she had stolen enough money to be able to sleep. Without lots of money in her bed, rest was impossible for her.

Mr Broombridge's first chore the next morning was to revisit the clothing store. He spent a good hour in front of the full-length mirror wanting to look the best he could for his beloved countess. He finally selected a silky blue suit and coordinating shirt and tie, with shiny black shoes completing the outfit.

Any astute observer would have noticed that Mr Broombridge approached the change room cubicle with extreme caution and trepidation, even insisting that a salesperson go in first to check that it wasn't already occupied. On the way out, resplendent in his new outfit, he spotted a beautiful hand-stitched leather briefcase that he felt added the final professional touch to his sartorial splendour.

Mr Broombridge and his countess spent the entire afternoon at the lawyer's office preparing a proposed last will and testament for Johann and his wife, Anna.

'If they sign this,' one of the lawyers exclaimed, 'they must really love you a lot!'

'Oh, yes! Oh, yes!' Kunnikunde sniffed, turning on the waterworks. 'I'm the most loved person in the family.' She placed her hand on her heart. 'Love! Love! My darling family!' Mr Broombridge handed her a silk handkerchief, and she demurely dabbed her eyes. Kunnikunde's heartfelt love suddenly turned to hateful impatience. 'Now! Hurry up and give Mr Broombridge the papers!' she snarled.

When they eventually left the lawyer's office, Kunnikunde strode out with a triumphant look on her face. Entering the elevator down to the lobby her triumph turned to intense excitement. 'I can't wait to eradicate that awful family of mine!' she hissed, raising her arms and acting out the evil deed she couldn't wait to perform. Big mistake! With her left arm, she accidentally released a laser bomb. It exploded with a huge bang and flash, lighting up the elevator just as it reached the ground floor. The blast blew the doors off, and thick black smoke poured out, filling the lobby. The smoke immediately triggered the smoke alarms, setting off the sprinkler system. Chaos and panic ensued. In the mayhem, few, if any, noticed the two blackened figures staggering from the elevator, their hair on fire. Luckily, the sprinklers quickly extinguished the flames. As a fully-fledged hell witch, burning hair was a mere inconvenience for Kunnikunde, who was heard to shriek, 'I'll be back!' before disappearing into thin air.

For the very human Mr Broombridge, however, his hair catching on fire was a major catastrophe. Even though the showering sprinklers quickly extinguished it, he only managed to stagger a few paces from the elevator before collapsing in a heap on the floor.

25

In Snobtown, Kunnikunde's daughters Pink and Rose were watching a live TV show about the presidential nomination, which had been dubbed 'The New Colony Has No Talent.' The show had only been running for a few minutes when the sisters heard a crashing sound coming from their mother's study. Rushing in, they found Kunnikunde slumped in her chair, her hair smouldering.

Pink grabbed a nearby vase and tipped its flowers and water over her mother's head, dousing any leftover flames. With her fierce eyes peering out from her drenched, charcoal face, Kunnikunde screeched, 'Lucifer! It must have been Lucifer who set me on fire! He's jealous of my success because he's such a loser himself! He's trying to sabotage me! But I'm tough! Very tough! I'll show him!'

Several hours later, after a very long shower, some heavily applied makeup and a bottle-blonde wig, Kunnikunde started to look like herself again.

At about this time, Mr Broombridge woke up in a hospital bed with his head heavily bandaged and dressings on his multiple minor burns. The flames had consumed his hair and singed his eyebrows.

'What happened?' he gurgled, trying to sit up. 'And where is my beautiful new suit?' he demanded of the attending nurse.

'Your suit didn't survive the bomb attack,' the nurse said. 'And you were extremely lucky to survive it yourself, Mr Broombridge.'

Poor Broombridge groaned and slumped back onto the bed in shock.

When staff at the clothing store opened the doors the next morning, they were greeted by a heavily bandaged man in a hospital gown and slippers making a beeline for the men's suit department. As he went by, they heard him say, 'I'll be charging this suit to the company!'

Sometime later he left the store with a new suit, shoes, briefcase, and several shirts and ties, and headed straight to his hair stylist. After judicious makeup to cover his burns, false eyebrows and a toupee, he almost felt like himself again.

That afternoon the old Ritter von Krumm pencil company had a board meeting, without their boss, where Rollover von Cracklingen and Count Farty Ritter von Krumm put a motion to remove Countess Kunnikunde as head of the company.

'What? No! How dare you!' Mr Broombridge shouted with horror and disgust. 'This is profoundly insulting to our beloved countess and leader! And deeply offensive to me! Kunnikunde and I plan to strip all our managers of any decision-making powers and enforce total control ourselves.'

'That is absolutely the wrong idea!' retorted a frustrated Rollover. 'Farty and I want to turn the clock back and empower our teams to have initiative and become creative and competitive again!'

'Just look at the numbers!' Farty shouted. 'We're heading straight for bankruptcy!'

'You fools!' an angry Broombridge shouted back. 'Total top-down control! No staff input to decision-making! Executive control only! Control! And more control! It's the only way out of this dire situation!'

Rollover and Farty's hope of gaining Mr Broombridge's support was shattered. They could almost hear the sound of the chisel etching the once iconic company's demise date on its headstone.

'Because of our glorious leader, Countess Kunnikunde Ritter von Krumm, our great company will soon be twice its size!' Broombridge proclaimed. 'You'll see!'

An angry, frustrated Rollover von Cracklingen had a sudden urge to kill something and ran out of the meeting to go hunting. Farty Ritter von Krumm simply wandered off home; he'd been in the office almost half the day and that was more than enough effort for the week. In complete contrast, Mr Broombridge spent the rest of the day having to retype the last will and testament of Johann and Anna Ritter von Krumm because the originals were damaged in the elevator explosion.

Back at university, Andy was busy helping treat sick and injured animals. Today was quite a significant one because he was to perform his first knee reconstruction on an old dog, under the watchful eye of Professor Katz-Kopf.

Once he had successfully completed the procedure, the professor congratulated him. 'I'm extremely impressed with you, Dolittle,' he said. 'I don't know anyone who could have done better!'

Andy was pleased with himself but didn't tell his professor that he had the great advantage of a fantastic gift for getting a quick and accurate diagnosis—the ability to see through the fur and skin of animals without the need for x-rays. Also, his hands were steady and unbelievably fast. Andy performed the knee reconstruction on the dog in a third of the time it would have taken a fully-trained veterinary surgeon. Professor Katz-Kopf became so used to Andy's extraordinary skills that nothing his remarkable student did surprised him anymore . . . well, almost nothing. The one exception was when he suggested to Andy that he begin writing a paper about joints and their medical history and procedures, which he would need as part of his qualifications for becoming a veterinary surgeon. The next morning Andy handed the dumbfounded professor a three-hundred-page document on the required topic.

'Dolittle!' Professor Katz-Kopf cried. 'You're supposed to take a couple of years to write this paper—not one day!'

'Oh! Sorry, Professor,' Andy said, reaching out his hand to take the document back.

'Not so fast, Dolittle!' he retorted. 'I'll hold onto it! I shall correct this work of haste myself. . . . I want to know what goes on in your hyperactive brain! I'll get back to you.'

Andy just shrugged his shoulders. 'By the way Professor, I won't be attending university tomorrow as I have an important family meeting.'

'With your parents?' the professor asked.

'No,' Andy responded impulsively, 'with a killer aunt . . . um . . . sorry, aunt!'

A killer ant? the professor thought but didn't dare ask.

Picking up the professor's medical bag, Andy left his mentor shaking his head and strolled towards the zoo. Soon after he got there, he performed a tooth extraction on a hyena using only local anesthetic—any other vet would have needed to put the animal asleep first. They were all well aware that hyenas have exceptionally powerful jaws and extremely aggressive natures.

Following the tooth extraction, Andy inspected numerous other animals, including a lion cub, a seal and a young giraffe. The animals' loving attitude towards Andy was still a source of amazement for the zookeepers, who never tired of seeing it.

That night, as requested by Michaela, Andy stayed in the big barn apartment next to his home.

'Our situation has eased a lot,' she announced as soon as Andy arrived by teleportation. 'It seems your Aunt Kunnikunde has rid herself of the powerful and evil black cloud spirit over her head. She is now incapable of detecting any spiritual phenomena herself.' Michaela then produced a small white pebble. 'Andy, hold this in your hand and say three times "I love you, my dearest aunt!"'

A bemused Andy obliged. Seconds later, Michaela disappeared. She reappeared half an hour later, rolling her eyes and grumbling. 'Your father can be a very stubborn and nervous man,' she complained. 'Unbelievable!' But she seemed pleased, nonetheless.

26

Early the next morning, Mr Broombridge returned to his observation hideout opposite Andy's house, keen to report the arrival of Johann and Anna to Countess Kunnikunde. With most of his bandages removed, his toupée firmly in place and false eyebrows securely glued on he almost looked like his normal self. Dressed in red trousers—a Teutonian status symbol—combined with an elegant leather jacket, he could not help regularly admiring himself in the personal mirror he carried with him at all times.

As Mr Broombridge gazed approvingly at his reflection, Andy and Michaela were focused on foiling Kunnikunde's plan to assassinate the family. They left the barn and went straight to the house and upstairs to Anna and Johann's private living room. Michaela immediately activated her three magic robotic pebbles, which instantly transformed into robot clones of Johann, Anna and Andy. Fake Johann was dressed in pyjamas and fake Anna in a nightgown.

'That's what your parents were wearing when I visited them last night,' Michaela explained. 'We'll have to dress these clones in proper clothes.'

This proved to be quite an involved job for Michaela, trying to choose suitable outfits from Anna and Johann's wardrobes on her own, because Andy was absolutely no help in that department. Besides, he was too distracted by his clone. He was in awe of the similarity, although there was no similarity whatsoever in their power of speech. The only thing coming out of his clone's mouth was, 'I love you, my dearest aunt!' However, he was amazed by how convincing it looked and sounded.

Once the robot clones were properly attired, Michaela added their final touches, which mostly involved putting lipstick and make-up on fake Anna. Finally happy with her creations, Michaela had the robots sit down and then she switched them off. She pointed out the window. 'Now I have to put our spy over there in the forest to sleep for a while, so he'll think he missed the arrival of your parents.' She laughed. 'We are all set for phase one!'

Half a minute later, Michaela appeared behind Mr Broombridge, who was sitting in the forest watching the house through his binoculars. She touched him on the back, and he fell into an instant, deep sleep.

Meanwhile, in Snobtown, the evil Countess Kunnikunde had happily prepared herself for what she fully expected to be a hugely triumphant day. At last, I will be rid of that horrid family of mine once and for all! she told herself. Dressed all in black, she took her small suitcase, packed with essentials for the next few days, downstairs to the sitting room and waited impatiently for Mr Broombridge's call.

After hearing nothing from him for two hours, the countess lost her patience and zapped herself and the suitcase to his camp hideout. To her consternation, she found her normally grovelling servant sound asleep. To say she was angry did not begin to describe her fury. 'You rotten little creep!' she screeched, swinging her suitcase in a great arc, clobbering poor Mr Broombridge in the head with it. 'Incompetent dunce! Can't I rely on anyone anymore?'

This tactic could have knocked Broombridge from mere sleep to total unconsciousness. Somehow, however, his head coped with the blow. The same couldn't be said for his toupée, which had partly dislodged and now hung down over his eyes. He woke up with a bewildered grunt of pain, followed by a yelp of alarm when he thought there was some hairy forest creature on his face.

'Urrrrgh!' he cried, violently brushing whatever it was off him. His toupée went flying and landed in a bush behind him. Then he saw the livid face of his beloved countess glaring at him. 'Sorry! Sorry!' he squealed, cowering before her, his hands up to his face in self-defence. 'I must have dozed off!'

Kunnikunde pushed her watch close to his face. 'Look at the time . . . you good-for-nothing!' she shrieked. 'I've been waiting more than two hours!'

Fumbling for his binoculars, the now bald and deeply embarrassed Mr Broombridge tried to make good while Kunnikunde continued to shout at him. Through the binocular lenses, he saw something that made him jump up and down, yelping with delight. There, as large as life on the front porch of their house, were Johann, Anna and Andy. 'Good news, my Countess!' he cried with glee. 'They have just arrived!' Suddenly he took the binoculars from his face and looked at Kunnikunde with concern. 'But our appointment is not for another half an hour,' he whined.

'I don't need an appointment . . . you failing fool!' Kunnikunde screeched at him, her eyes scrunched shut and her face red with rage. 'I AM the appointment! Now! Let's go, you idiotic imbecile! Move!'

They rushed to Broombridge's car and roared off, arriving minutes later in front of Andy's house. Andy greeted them at the front door. 'Welcome, dear Aunt Kunnikunde!' he said with a beaming smile. 'Long time, no see!'

Kunnikunde tried to return the smile, but it ended up being more a grimace of anger and hate. 'Your parents are in?' she demanded to know.

'Of course, Aunty! They are waiting for you in the living room.'

Kunnikunde brushed past Andy and rushed into the house, making a beeline for the living room. There, to her delight and relief, sitting on the sofa and smiling up at her were Johann and Anna. Finally! she thought to herself, unaware they were robot versions of the real thing. Now nothing is stopping me from eliminating them! She immediately strode over to fake Johann and Anna and shook their hands, smiling sweetly. Suddenly she had a short burst of panic. Her sweet smile turned into a toothy snarl as she yelled at Mr Broombridge, 'Where's the boy? Why isn't he here?'

'Coming!' a voice called out from the kitchen. Fake Andy walked in and sat down next to his parents. 'I love you, my dearest Aunt!' he chirped.

This elicited a grunt of disapproval from fake Johann. 'I don't like you, Kunnikunde!' he blurted out.

Kunnikunde seemed unperturbed, until fake Anna spoke. 'Would you like a cup of tea, Kunnikunde?' she asked sweetly.

She might as well have asked 'Would you like a glass of cyanide?' for the effect it had on the evil countess. It triggered an explosion of jealousy and rage.

'You creepy witch!' she shrieked at Anna, her eyes flashing with hate. 'Always happy and content . . . and so nice and polite it makes me sick! You shall be first!' With a sadistic grin, she stretched her arms out in front of her, pointed her hands directly at Anna and unleashed a barrage of fire bolts. Her arms were jolting back and forth at a rapid rate like a canon recoiling, accompanied by her hysterically happy laughter.

The living room quickly filled with thick black smoke, but Kunnikunde kept shooting her fire bolts. When she finally stopped, she couldn't see a thing. The only sound, apart from her own heavy breathing, was Mr Broombridge choking on the smoke.

'Imbecile!' she screeched at him. 'Open the door!'

As the smoke began dispersing, the devastating force of Kunnikunde's firepower was clear to see. Its destructive capacity even surprised Kunnikunde herself. There was nothing left of the sofa or the people who had been occupying it. The curtains were on fire, the rug was smouldering, and the entire room was blackened.

'I have done it!' Kunnikunde shrieked with joy. 'I have finally eliminated that disgusting family! I have done what Lucifer himself could not do! I'm the greatest! I'm the toughest!'

She turned to Mr Broombridge and saw that he was as blackened as everything else in the room, and then realised she was too. 'Quickly, you good-for-nothing!' she shrieked. 'Let's go! We don't want to be seen!' They raced out to the car and roared off with Kunnikunde in the driver's seat. 'You'll have to report this terrible accident to the police!' she commanded Mr Broombridge.

27

On the way back to the hotel, Kunnikunde couldn't stop giggling. To Mr Broombridge, it sounded like the cackling of a demented witch at her cauldron. While the countess thought it was possibly the happiest day of her life, Broombridge was trembling with the shock of having witnessed brutal, cold-blooded murder.

Back at the house, Andy watched Kunnikunde and Broombridge drive away then sounded the 'all clear' to Michaela. She immediately rushed into the living room and waved her right hand in a big circle. A bright blue flash lit up the house and everything returned to normal. Actually, the room was better than normal—all the curtains and furnishings looked brand new.

There were also three shiny white pebbles on the sofa. When Michaela picked them up, Andy was wide-eyed with astonishment.

'Are they still working?' he gasped.

'Of course! You can't kill spirit robots!'

About an hour later, police cars and fire trucks began arriving at the house, their sirens blaring. As expected, the first one to storm inside was Police Commander Wurstling.

'We had a report of a terrorist attack and a fire engulfing your house!' he shouted excitedly. Rather than a fire, it was his excitement that was quickly extinguished. After a rapid investigation of the house, he bellowed to his police officers and firefighters who were rushing in the front door, 'False alarm! False alarm! Everything is normal!'

Knowing what Anna would do, Michaela served tea and biscuits to the police squad and fire crew. Commander Wurstling politely declined the tea but accepted a glass of schnapps. At that point, Hermann and Fritz arrived home from work and immediately prepared large platters of freshly cut vegetables and air-dried meat. That inspired Michaela to show her culinary talents by serving up beautiful cheese plates.

The false alarm lasted until late that night.

In the hotel the next morning, Countess Kunnikunde woke up as happy as it was possible for her to be. She was chirpy instead of snarly and couldn't stop smiling. Mr Broombridge had never seen her this way . . . ever.

As happy as she was, Kunnikunde was still focused on the task at hand and its unfinished business.

'Broombridge!' She was somehow able to yell and smile at the same time. 'Have you made the court appointment for me to launch proceedings for my dear departed brother-in-law's last will and testament?' She had asked him this repeatedly, even though Mr Broombridge had confirmed that he had made the appointment and it was that same afternoon. He put it down to her excitement at the thought of getting into the courtroom and finalising the will.

Even the news that Rollover von Cracklingen and Farty Ritter von Krumm were planning a coup against her couldn't put a dampener on her ebullient mood.

She giggled like a little girl, saying, 'I shall simply fire them!'

Kunnikunde and Mr Broombridge checked the morning newspapers and TV bulletins to see if their dastardly deed was reported.

'No mention of it,' Mr Broombridge grumbled. 'I definitely informed them all.'

The countess laughed. 'You just informed them too late for it to make this morning's news, dearest Broombridge! We have to wait for the afternoon bulletins! They will be full of my triumphant success! I can see the headline now! TRAGIC DEATH OF FAMILY IN HOUSE FIRE. Hi! Hi! Hi! Hi!' she sang as she danced towards the elevator to take her to her room to dress for her important court appearance. Kunnikunde couldn't bring herself to imagine a headline that read, TRAGIC DEATH OF FAMOUS AND WELL-RESPECTED FAMILY IN HOUSE FIRE.

Mr Broombridge hurried back to his favourite clothing store to buy a black suit befitting the occasion.

It seemed most citizens of Stone were interested in the proceedings because the courtroom was packed to overflowing. Presiding Judge Helmut Richter observed this with dismay as he took his place at his table. Processing last wills and testaments was the one aspect of his job he disliked intensely.

Andy and Michaela snuck into the courtroom and sat in the back row. Michaela had disguised Andy as a middle-aged man. 'This is what you will look like when you are fifty!' she gleefully told him.

Just as Judge Richter was calming the hubbub in the courtroom in preparation to commence proceedings, the door burst open. In stormed a woman dressed all in black, her face obscured behind a black lace veil. 'I don't deserve this inheritance!' she wailed. 'I don't really want it! But he loved me! He loved me so very much! To refuse it would dishonour my dear brother-in-law!' She marched right up to the judge's table, slammed her papers down in front of him and took a seat in the first row, together with Mr Broombridge.

Taken aback, the judge quickly composed himself. 'And who might you be?' he asked, trying to be civil.

'I am no other than the Countess Kunnikunde Ritter von Krumm!' Kunnikunde replied, half sobbing half choking in an attempt to sound grief-stricken.

Judge Richter seemed not to have noticed. 'That's funny,' he said, studying Kunnikunde's papers. 'This morning a young lady lodged a new will and testament on behalf of Count Johann Ritter von Krumm that supersedes yours . . . and there was no mention of you in it. So, I'm very happy to tell you that you no longer have to worry about accepting something you don't really want. You must be very relieved that the matter is of no more concern to you. You can go home now.'

The judge's gavel banged down on its block and the case was closed—at least Judge Richter thought it was.

Both Mr Broombridge and Kunnikunde were on their feet, utterly confused and very angry.

'This is theft!' screeched Kunnikunde. 'It's my money! My house! My company! Mine, all mine!'

'Show me the police report!' Broombridge shouted.

'Should there be a police report?' retorted the now agitated Judge Richter.

'Of course, there should, you incompetent fool!' Broombridge yelled.

That was a mistake.

'Sir! . . . you will leave this courtroom now! There is no police report because there is nothing to report. As far as this court is concerned, Count Johann and his family are well and truly alive!'

'Idiot!' shouted an enraged Broombridge. He pointed at his beloved countess. 'She killed them! I saw it with my own eyes! I'm a witness! That family has been obliterated!'

WHACK! The countess hit Mr Broombridge hard—so hard that one of the laser bombs hidden in her sleeve slipped out and rolled towards the judge's table.

Mr Broombridge saw it first and started running . . . but too late! The explosion lifted him in the air. A nanosecond later, the judge's table was blown to smithereens. The judge was launched skywards feet first, his legs in a tangle. By the time he crashed back down onto the remains of his table, the courtroom was filled with black smoke.

The aftershock of the explosion brought an eerie silence, finally broken by Kunnikunde's hysterical, ear-piercing scream. 'You are fired, Broombridge! You are fired!' she yelled before disappearing into thin air.

Judge Richter dragged himself to his feet, in shock. He was slightly bruised but otherwise unhurt.

Predictably, poor Mr Broombridge wasn't so lucky. He ended up in the hospital with a broken arm and minor burns to his body. Fortunately, no one else in the courtroom was physically injured . . . but the mental trauma of what they had witnessed was clearly evident on many faces.

28

In escaping the courtroom, Kunnikunde had used up the last teleportation the devil had granted her. She crashed down in her landing chair back at her office in Snobtown, blackened by the explosion and utterly confused. 'What happened?' she cried. 'Who would be so devious and dishonest as to falsify a will? Could it have been Rollover and Farty trying to steal from me? Or Lucifer himself . . . so insanely jealous of my success?' The distraught Kunnikunde continued to ask herself questions until Lucifer suddenly walked through the wall and stood before her.

'Kunnikunde!' he scolded, shaking his head. 'When will you learn to heed my advice?'

'You are just jealous that I achieved what you could not!' hissed the countess defiantly.

'Oh, yes!' laughed the devil. 'Underestimating a warrior spirit and killing three robots! What a success! I'm insanely jealous! Ha! Ha! Ha!'

'What?' screamed Kunnikunde. 'I killed that dreadful family! I saw it with my own eyes! I did it—not you! You can't take that away from me!'

'Yes, I can!' snarled the devil. 'It was you who refused the help of the spirit in the black cloud! It would have immediately recognised nasty little spirit robots like those you tried to kill.

Kunnikunde started to tremble with rage and frustration. 'No! No! No!' she howled. 'Who would be so cruel as to deceive me in that way?'

'An angel!' the devil snarled, almost choking on the word. 'The boy's guardian angel! At least, that's what you humans call them!'

Without warning, he touched Kunnikunde's hand, and in a flash, they were at the big city zoo where Andy was treating the eye of a brown bear as his girlfriend Sophia watched.

'Ohhhh!' Gasped Kunnikunde in disbelief. 'That's my nephew! The obnoxious little rat is alive! Let me kill him now!'

'No!' Lucifer snapped. 'He's too strong! And your power is now far too weak to harm him. I can't believe that my spirit enemies would pass on such powers to a useless soul trapped in flesh and blood! It's a first in the history of the universe!'

ZAP! The devil and Kunnikunde were back in Snobtown.

'But at least I killed his horrible father and creepy mother!' Kunnikunde cried triumphantly.

When Lucifer told her they too had been spirit robots, denying the countess any success, she lost her dignity completely. Lucifer vanished in a puff of smoke as Kunnikunde went into total meltdown. Extreme hate, anger and self-pity had finally driven Kunnikunde out of her mind. Her daughters had no choice but to call an ambulance to take her to an insane asylum, where she stayed for many months.

After reading Andy's rushed paper on joints at least ten times, Professor Katz-Kopf couldn't fault it and had it published as an exemplary work.

Even though he was only in his second year of veterinary studies, Andy performed like a fully-fledged doctor. He operated on various animals with brilliant surgical skills and was superb in diagnosing any ailments his patients suffered from. His girlfriend Sophia was a frequent visitor to Andy's house and was quickly becoming part of the family. Johann began to smell the sweet, intoxicating fruit of retirement and started promoting people within his company to ease his own workload and take over from him when he finally called it a day.

Michaela went back into her magic pencil and did not materialise again until a year later when something totally unexpected happened—but that's another story.

Illustrations by Caroline Webb

www.ingramcontent.com/pod-product-compliance
Lightning Source LLC
LaVergne TN
LVHW011722060526
838200LV00051B/2999
9780228880882